PAST THREE O'CLOCK

The Story of Sebelius Sallow

Richie Joyce

PAST THREE O'CLOCK

May your bird be well stuffed and your pigs snuggly nestled in their blankets. Love always

Richie Joyce

Past Three O'Clock

Published by Little Robin Red Press

Copyright © Richie Joyce 2024

Hardback ISBN: 978-0-9565579-1-9
Paperback ISBN: 978-0-9565579-2-6
eBook ISBN: 978-0-9565579-3-3

Editor: Paul Swallow

Cover illustration and design: Lex Goodwin

Typesetting and formatting: The Book Typesetters

The right of Richie Joyce to be identified as the author of this work has been asserted by him in accordance with the Copyright, Designs and Patents Act 1988.

You may not copy, store, distribute, transmit, reproduce or otherwise make available this publication (or any part of it) in any form, or by any means (electronic, digital, optical, mechanical, photocopying, recording or otherwise), without the prior written permission of the publisher.

Any person who does any unauthorised act in relation to this publication may be liable to criminal prosecution and civil claims for damages.

A CIP catalogue record for this book is available from the British Library.

This book is a work of fiction. Names, characters, places, and incidents are either the product of the author's imagination or are used fictitiously. Any resemblance to actual persons, living or dead, events, or locales is entirely coincidental.

Disclaimer: The views expressed in this book are solely those of the author and do not necessarily reflect the official policy or position of any organisation or individual mentioned within.

Every effort has been made to ensure the accuracy of the information presented in this book; however, the author and the publisher assume no responsibility for errors, omissions, or damages arising from the use of the information contained herein.

Past Three O'Clock

The Story of Sebelius Sallow

Richie Joyce

THIS
CHRISTMAS BOOK
IS CORDIALLY INSCRIBED TO ANY
WHO HAVE NEVER THOUGHT ME AN
INCONVENIENCE

But especially...

Mam and Dad for blessing me with the best life

Andrew, who completes my world and always strives to make it a happy one

Cheryl, for gifting me, and the universe, the greatest person I could have ever imagined having

Julian and Claire, thank you for William. Life would be a dismal place without him

Foreword

I decided that I would pen the story of Sebelius Sallow on December 4, 2023 — a significant date, marking the thirty-third anniversary of my grandmother's passing, an event that forever shaped my life. It took another thirteen days before I began writing on that cold Saturday morning in December. Inspired by the speed with which Mr Dickens wrote my favourite book, *A Christmas Carol*, I wanted to create my own story.

So monumental was the man in question, he cemented his name to an era that already had been labelled. While Queen Victoria's long reign defined the period as the Victorian age, it was Dickens, through the term 'Dickensian', who magnificently exposed the social classes, institutions, injustices, laws, protocols, pageantry, and tragedies of the time.

My love for Queen Victoria, her husband, and the age they shaped began before I had conscious memory. Having been introduced to the period at some point, with little recollection of the exact time, I remember the strong parallels through my own upbringing. This began with my own grandmother. She was my queen and I her faithful subject. After losing her husband quite suddenly, she descended into a permanent state of mourning. They had raised seven children and were blessed with eighteen grandchildren, not all of whom my grandfather got to meet. From the moment I was born, I became my grandmother's constant companion. Despite having such a large family, she desperately longed to be with the man who left this world against his will and long before his time — he always injected life into any situation. She, in turn, would have sacrificed anything to keep him by her side. This is an homage to everything and everyone I love.

Charles Dickens penned his tale of Ebenezer Scrooge in just six weeks, while I wrote my tale of Sebelius Sallow in a disappointing sixty-three days, with an additional thirty-five days required for editing. All in all, ninety-eight days to create *my* ghostly little Christmas book, of which I am terribly proud, is not bad going. Mr Dickens created his masterpiece under severe financial constraints but had the luxury of taking nighttime strolls and three-mile expeditions on horseback. Although I have no monetary issues of my own, I work full time in a busy call centre, having other people's voices in my head around 97.8% of the time.

I am no Charles Dickens — to which I know I will be readily met with a resounding, "No, you most certainly are not!" That is not to say however, that I'm any less worthy as a human being, a writer and someone who has stories inside them that they yearn to get down in print.

This novella is sprinkled with 'Dickensianisms' that any ardent Dickens fan will recognise instantly. My best-loved is Patty Cake's exchange with Colonel Cecil-Yule, inspired by the exquisite scene from *The Old Curiosity Shop*, where Mr Swiveller scrutinises Mr Cheggs in a contemptuous, mocking manner. If you're familiar with this scene, I hope you'll appreciate my homage. If not, I urge you to delve into the eighth chapter of that Dickens masterpiece.

Many aspects inspired the story of Sebelius Sallow: naturally, Dickens himself, the queen who ruled and became a mother — albeit an absent one, at times — to her nation, my own wonderful family, and my love of Christmas and the carols that enhance it.

This brings me nicely to the Christmas carol, 'Past Three O'Clock', which inspired me to weave it into my own story, not only for its beautiful melody, that plays from the clock that Sebelius created, but for the fascinating origins of its own creation. The carol itself had not in fact been written during the time of Sebelius Sallow, but the melody certainly existed.

In 1924, exactly one hundred years ago, the English Anglican priest, George Ratcliffe Woodward, put his poetic and musical talents to good use when he published a collection of hymns and carols. Among them was one which was to become a favourite of mine, 'Past Three O'Clock'. Reverend Woodward's text was set to music by composer Charles Wood, using the exact melody of the traditional medieval tune 'London Waits.' The lyrics penned by the clergyman proclaimed the birth of Christ and the joy of the season, yet presented in the style of traditional watchman's cry. This was the call heard in the streets of old London as night watchmen announced the hours.

People have asked me, why Sebelius Sallow? It's the name I give to that flicker of a shadow caught at the periphery of sight. I have always believed it's not merely a trick of the light, but Sebelius Sallow. It's not for me to prove myself right, but for you to prove me wrong, and I invite you to try.

I am extremely proud to publish this work as an independent author and to stand alongside the many talented indie authors I am privileged to know. There is a stigma surrounding us, as if those who are traditionally published were chosen for a team while we were picked last or not chosen at all. However, I see us very much like my heroes — Vincent Van Gogh, Paul Cézanne, and Toulouse-Lautrec — who created their art according to their own vision, never bowing down or limiting their ideas by those who believe they know better. They painted authentically, with all the imperfections on show — warts (or missing ears) and all.

This is the third book I've written, but the first I am publishing myself. Now that I have taken this step, I plan to publish my other works in the coming years. With no children to leave in the world beyond my time, my words will be my legacy.

Preface

The only spirits that truly fade are those whose names are never spoken, whose memories never live on in any mind, and whose deeds do not warm the hearts of those left behind. May we all go forth in life so that our spirits never fade.

I pray we stop and acknowledge all the Sebelius Sallows that live amongst us. They are all around us. Cherish them.

Wishing you all the merriment of Christmas, not just at this joyous time, but all the year through.

Your festive friend,

R.J.

December, 2024

Prologue

Who...?
   Sebelius Sallow.
I shall ask you again.
Do you know of Sebelius Sallow?
No? I don't suppose you do, or that you would attest to it.

I would have to say that if you were questioned in a court of law, you would swear on the sanctity of the Bible that you do not know, nor have ever seen, Sebelius Sallow. And I, not wishing to be the bearer of bad news at this festive time, take no delight in declaring your perjury, because we have all, at one time or another, had the pleasure or displeasure of our dealings with the aforementioned man.

Now, don't be afraid.

Sebelius Sallow was the most gentle of God's creatures, and certainly was a man that was the physical embodiment of his name. When he was alive, and I say this because he has long since passed, but, when he was alive he was individual in his appearance and most singular in his ways. I will do my absolute best to describe him as no known portrait or image survives of him today.

Think about Sebelius Sallow. How would he look to you?

You might imagine a man named Sebelius to be tall, slender as a stick and as straight-bodied a man as you ever did see, like a scarecrow. Not to say he looked as dishevelled as a scarecrow. No, you might see him as square-shouldered, a long face and nose with slightly large nostrils, and a walk that gave him an air of stiffness in his manner — and you would be correct.

His surname, Sallow, aptly matched his chalky complexion, but don't be put off, his manner was always pleasant and mild. Regardless of these features, he was very agreeable to look at. If you were to liken him to an inanimate object, you might say he likened a window.

Why a window?

We see windows every day — day in, day out. We see, but we do not observe. A window doesn't elicit any real emotion, unless it is a true thing of beauty, like the kind you see in a church or cathedral, then we might stop and stare, because those windows captivate us with their intricate shapes, ever changing colour and magnificent detail, we simply find it hard to look away.

No, Sebelius Sallow would be the plainest of windows, and the only excitement to be derived from a boring window is the eagerness to look beyond the pane of glass, to inspect what is happening inside.

That was Sebelius Sallow.

All those around him would look through him, carrying on with their endeavours and paying no attention to his presence.

They always looked beyond him.

I

London, 1836

It was precisely 3:00 p.m. on this cold, snowy Saturday afternoon. The bright white sky hung over the City of London like an enormous grubby pillow, and it showed no sign of surrendering to the perishing darkness of evening.

It was the seventeenth day of December, and, inside the little clock shop, the endless ticking and tocking was drowned out by the delights of the bing-bonging, ding-donging, ringing and bringing, ting-tinging and the cuckooing as nigh on two-hundred watches, clocks and timepieces, small and large, old and new, chimed in and out of sequence as they verified the hour.

In front of the large window, Sebelius positioned himself at the counter, making good use of the light of the intensely fleecy sky, a pair of long-nosed tweezers gripped in his thin fingers. Intrinsically poised, he held his breath as the final adjustments were made to the most beautiful and intricate clock in the entire shop, his masterpiece.

"There. Now you are complete, my friend," he said, allowing a modest smile to meet his face.

The shop once more hummed with the merry rhythm of its

tick-tocking, as though in this little place beat the very heart of London.

Staring hard in contemplation as to how he might turn over the excellently carved, yet hefty timepiece, that had to be thirty-five inches in diameter, his concentration was broken by the sound of the bell that hung above the door.

"Greetings of the season!" exclaimed his customer who stepped in removing his hat, shaking it in the open doorway to remove the fine flakes of snow.

"Forgive me," Sebelius replied in his awkward manner, "we are closed. In my absent mindedness I did not turn the sign and fasten the door."

"I do beg your pardon—" the gentleman said apologetically, closing the door and making no effort to move back through it.

Sebelius, understanding the complex runnings of even the most delicate of timepieces, found the workings of mankind extremely difficult. The misinterpretation of unspoken gestures and the cues of appropriateness were often lost on him; instead, these were replaced with painful feelings of immense awkwardness when in the company of others; generally he found solace in his own company and in the repetition of routine. The same thing, day in day out, brought its own consolation.

It was for this reason he found his affinity with time. Time did nothing but repeat its function every second, moving in the same circular motion, never tiring or finding itself in want of changing direction. That was Sebelius Sallow — he was as complex as the innermost workings of the most involute timepiece.

A sigh passed his lips. "How may I assist you?" he conceded with an attempt of a smile.

"Pardon me." His customer's eyes widened and his complexion warmed at the sight of the watchmaker's face. "Aren't you Sebelius Sallow?"

"The very same. How might I help you, sir?"

"You do not recognise me, do you?"

"You must excuse me, I am usually very good with faces but I cannot affirm knowing you, sir."

"You are still the same old Sebelius," the gentleman retorted and chuckled.

"I wouldn't consider being in my twenty-fifth year as particularly old," he said quite matter of factly.

"I was not being literal, *young* Sebelius. We are, after all, the same age, and I certainly do not consider myself to be old. I remember that I should never address you as Seb, for I know you disapprove of it."

The horologist paused and stared hard at the face of the man who stood before him. He looked deep into his eyes, another situation that made him feel terribly uneasy. The mutual connection of gaze was unnatural to him. His uneasiness thawed and his eyes softened, they locked firmly and comfortably on the piercing virescent eyes of, "Aubrey? Aubrey Bravington?"

"The very same," he said and smiled.

Aubrey Bravington, an old acquaintance from Sebelius's youth, had not lost any of his physical attributes, they now merely hid behind his perfectly maintained, yet thick flame-red auburn beard and hair, hair so much more plentiful now, much longer than it was in the depths of way back when.

"Do you wish to see me?" Sebelius asked hopefully.

"I come in want of a remedy for this." Bravington stretched his arm before him, his fist tightly gripping a chain which graced the most splendid gold pocket watch.

Sebelius was immediately dazzled by its beauty as it swung before him, like a pendulum in perfect time. This was not your run-of-the-mill pocket watch.

"May I?" He sought permission to inspect the piece.

Bravington handed it carefully to him without delay, and Sebelius held the precious article with the careful touch of an expert. After inspecting its physical artistry, the horologist went to work, like a Doctor of Medicine might assist a patient in the need of life-saving treatment.

First the heartbeat. Sebelius closed his eyes, putting his patient to his ear. He listened and sighed in exasperation upon making his diagnosis.

On the glass counter before him lay a rigid mat of leather, topped with a velvet sapphire cloth. He placed a pair of fine spectacles at the end of his protrusive nose and opened the timepiece. Immediately, the inscribed maker's mark leaped out and Sebelius knew his patient was an illustrious one.

Huffs and puffs were made while constructing a remedy, and, putting his tools of the trade to use, he went to work.

There was a sigh, and then a quick draw of breath.

He did not exhale.

On the surface, Aubrey Bravington was always as cool as the frozen Thames, yet his heart doubled in pace. He had thought to intervene or ask a question, but feared that a break in concentration might result in a fatal loss.

"And there you have it!" Sebelius said and then smiled.

Giving the treasure one last inspection, he closed his eyes tightly, pressed his patient to his ear and listened as its little heartbeat moved with a new unfaltering rhythmical flow.

"Past three o'clock," Sebelius whispered in delight, setting the time precisely and winding his patient back to health.

Bravington exhaled in delight as Sebelius set to work, making the pocket watch sparkle with his trusty polishing cloth.

Pulling out a sapphire velvet pouch, topped with a drawstring of gold, he entrusted the treasure in its safe keeping. The timepiece was then placed in a perfectly sized box, a blaze of sapphire upon which, in gold print, were inscribed the words: *Sallow of Ludgate Hill*. Below this it read: *Where seconds, minutes and hours are a gift*.

"You are a genius."

"And you, Aubrey, are lackadaisical," Sebelius remonstrated.

"Sebelius!" Bravington did not attempt to conceal the injury of his tone as he stared disappointedly at his friend.

"Anyone who has the good fortune to possess such a fine piece and then fails to have it routinely maintained, is negligent."

"My dear Sebelius, this is not my timepiece. I only wish it were. It belongs to the second Earl Grey. He is... my future father-in-law..." Bravington trailed off on seeing the deep hidden disappointment in his friend's eyes, but continued his painful explanation. "I am betrothed to his daughter, Georgiana Grey."

An uncomfortable pause loomed, broken only by the crackle of the fire upon the hearth.

Neither man spoke.

"I apologise. In that case, Earl Grey should take better care. Felicitations to you and your future wife."

"Have you been fortunate to find love?" Bravington asked.

Sebelius was still. "Who would have me?"

Again the uncomfortable silence.

"One day it will be you, Sebelius. I am sure of it."

"I am truly glad to hear of such cheery news, Aubrey. I am quite content as I am, thank you."

"You have not asked of me the same question, Sebelius."

"What question?"

"If I had been fortunate enough to find love."

"You speak such nonsense. You have stated your situation and—"

"My answer is: *no*. Ours is not a love match. My father desires this marriage. I am to inherit his fortune and he wishes to prepare me. My desire, as you know, is to be a portraitist, my easel is never without a commission. Earl Grey wishes me to go into Westminster and reform this country for the good of the people, but family comes first and so I am prepared for this life of political servitude."

"Aubrey, there are those in real servitude who would trade places with you in less than a second."

"That swiftly?"

Sebelius delivered a familiar look and went on to remind his visitor of the less fortunate people who existed all around them, gathering most plentifully in London, living in their genuine drudgery knowing only hard work, hunger and homelessness. Not to mention the cold.

Bowing his head, shame set in as Bravington silently reminded himself of his excellent fortune.

"You are to marry the daughter of the former premier of this country. The drudgery that you speak of adorns itself in shirts of silk and coats of velvet, bedecked with buttons of gold. We are far more fortunate than the masses," Sebelius reminded him.

Moving towards the counter, Bravington reached for his friend's hand which was pressed to the glass counter. Sebelius swiftly moved it away, and began to fidget nervously with the enormous masterpiece that he had completed moments before.

"What thing of beauty is this?" Bravington asked, concealing his embarrassment after the minor rejection.

"A pursuit that has saved me from idleness and sorrow."

"You constructed this?"

"It has kept me occupied in between customers, and I have worked night and day to complete it, in time for Christmas."

"Is it for sale?"

"I couldn't possibly part with it. It has been a labour of love. I intended it to hang there." Sebelius pointed to the only available wall space above the fireplace, as the rest of the little shop was filled to the brim with every kind of timepiece imaginable. All of which were available to purchase, save this.

"Would you like a helping hand to put it in its place?"

"I would like that very much. I am not built for brute strength, as you know, and now it's complete, it's rather weighty."

They both suspended the hefty creation, with Bravington taking most of the weight, and so it was attached to the fixing on the wall.

"Wait! I have not set it to time. What is the hour?" Sebelius inquired, stumbling over his words nervously, his senses muddled by Bravington's intoxicating scent of lemon, lime, and bergamot, which lingered delicately atop a foundation of sandalwood, cedarwood, and musk.

His friend indicated with a grin and a nod that the shop was a mass of clocks all set precisely to time. "Take your pick."

Sebelius smiled and a flush of colour glowed in his pallid complexion. Aubrey Bravington possessed a smile so captivating that it could make a turncoat of every member of the Queen's Guard to his will, should he desire it.

"It's past three o'clock," Bravington observed.

"Wait! Shush!" Sebelius silenced him. "Listen."

The clock chimed, not the Cambridge Quarters, the most popular chime of choice, but something quite different.

"I know that tune. That's—"

"'London Waits,'" Sebelius said wistfully.

"My favourite of all tunes."

"I remembered. If you were not humming it, then you were whistling it, and if you were not whistling it, then it was whirring around in your head." Sebelius attempted a smile while his sparkly brown eyes focussed on the thing that chimed great joy.

The pair remained still as it played merrily.

When it completed its tune, Sebelius moved the hand to the next hour so that it could be heard again.

Bravington watched briefly, observing his friend's insufficient, lengthy frame, thin, with no surplus flesh. Sebelius Sallow had not changed a bit. His head, which sat on a thin neck, was perfectly proportioned in shape, and his face was still ever so pleasing, with large bright eyes that occasionally sparkled, giving the momentary belief of fulfilment, just as they were doing now. His attire, in style and silhouette, was pleasantly outdated, ordinary but well kept — a dark mustard coat, cut in the older fashion, not clinging to the form as it should, with a double row of large metal buttons; black trousers, and shoes that had just recalled better days.

"Who cares for you now?" Bravington asked hopefully.

"I care for myself. Father sadly passed away in the spring. He always had an affinity with spring, which is not to say he did not cherish Christmas just as dearly. January and February were his least favoured months. He found January too dreary, as we transition from the joy of Christmas to the monotony of another twelve months." Bravington watched as Sebelius's face came alive, living a few moments in the time when his father existed to love him. "He regarded February as particularly dreadful, believing our Creator shared the sentiment, hence why it was spared the full thirty-one days."

"My sincere condolences. I knew you were both so very close." Bravington empathised with a solemn reticence, understanding the depth of his friend's sorrow at Sebelius having lost not just one parent, but both. Though he longed to offer comforting words, he chose silence, knowing it conveyed more than words ever could.

Sebelius's eyes scanned the room. "He was all I had after Mother died. The hours we spent within these four walls," he said reminiscently. "I still have much to learn, and long for his guidance so often. I still feel him, but it's not the same."

Fumbling for his hat and overcoat, Sebelius prepared to embrace the majesty of the snowy winter afternoon.

"Sebelius, may I call on you again? Next Saturday?" Bravington asked. They both moved towards the door to leave.

The watchmaker paused, a brief silence stretching into what felt like an eternity. "I would look forward to it. I do, however, close at midday, being Christmas Eve."

Bravington, reflecting on his friend's mention of Christmas Eve and immediately recalling that it was Sebelius's favourite day, abruptly halted in his tracks. In his haste, he clumsily turned on his heel, inadvertently blocking the exit and causing the equally awkward Sebelius to collide, head-on, into him.

"Surely, you are forgetting a small matter?" Bravington asked, steadying his friend, merely inches apart.

Sebelius gulped. "What small matter?"

They both stood, quite still, the pounding of their hearts deafening the ticking within the shop.

"We have not completed our transaction," Bravington reminded him.

"Have we not?"

"Here," Bravington replied, holding out a gold sovereign bearing the late King's effigy. "For your services in repairing Earl Grey's pocket watch."

"Think nothing of it, Aubrey. Besides, a sovereign is far too excessive, even for my service."

"Nonsense. Please take it, if not for me then with Earl Grey's compliments of the season."

The horologist resisted any further insistence, yet, undeterred, Bravington reached for Sebelius's hand, delicately unfurling his fingers to reveal the soft, slender palm. Placing the coin within, he closed Sebelius's hand into a fist, reminiscent of the way elderly relatives would sometimes do to children as if they were gifting them infinite riches, their grip hinting at a desire to crush bones.

"Buy something wonderful, or keep it, which I suspect you will. May it bring you luck if nothing else, dear sweet Sebelius," Bravington said, still clutching his fisted hand in both of his.

In a nervous flutter of angst, Sebelius extricated himself from his friend's captivating snare-like grip, made even more difficult while being held in his mesmerising gaze. Seeking an exit, he fumbled for the door handle behind his visitor and swiftly opened it, slipping out with a hurried dash.

The reassuring click of the key activating the lock was never quite enough to ease the horologist's mind; he braced himself for what inevitably followed. With a meticulousness that he hoped would calm his inner turmoil, Sebelius grasped the handle and rhythmically rattled it six times, each movement to the tune of his own voice: "Door is locked. Door is locked." And then another nine rattles to: "Couldn't get in, if I tried. Door is locked."

Bravington turned in the doorway in the hope that he and his friend might walk a little of the way together until their destinations would cause them to part, but Sebelius, lost in a deflated state of unease, succumbed to the urge to repeat the routine once more.

Aware that this unbreakable ritual required full concentration, Bravington left Sebelius to his custom as he muttered, "Season's greetings, Sebelius… and happy birthday, my dear, sweet friend."

By the time Sebelius was sufficiently convinced that his door was locked and he was ready to leave, Aubrey Bravington was nowhere in sight.

II

It would be a tremendous fib to say that the following Saturday looked any different from the last, with the same billowing white sky hanging brightly over London, doing Jack Frost's bidding with unyielding vigour. That part is true, but it was extraordinarily different in every way, for this day was the twenty-fourth day of December. It marked the arrival of Christmas Eve.

The days leading up to this moment, as this was, after all, Sebelius Sallow's favourite day of the year, were quite different. Since that moment, when the snow-dusted Aubrey Bravington had burst through the door of his little shop to the fanfare of that tinkling bell, the horologist could do nothing but think with excitement about seeing his friend again.

With a sense of delight, he gleefully tore the final days of December from his wall calendar, leaving him with just seven pages clinging on, their serrated edges gripping tightly until the cycle began anew.

The festive period was a busy time for all merchants, and Sebelius's shop saw a constant stream of customers seeking last-minute tokens of love and appreciation, embodied in the form of time.

As soon as he unlocked his shop on the Monday following Bravington's visit, the little establishment resonated with customers' delight exclaiming, "Isn't it magnificent?" and expressing similar platitudes, as his grand timepiece melodiously chimed every hour.

"Where do I know that tune?" some inquired.

"I know it, I just can't put my finger on it," echoed others in various forms of phrasing.

This inspired Sebelius to craft and mount a beautiful handwritten note beneath his timepiece which read:

If you have the pleasure of being present on the hour, lend an ear to the melody of 'London Waits' — a seasonal offering to you. Should you wish to convey your enjoyment, a contribution to the Clerkenwell Union workhouse would be deeply appreciated.

Kindness and thoughtfulness were forever at the forefront of his every endeavour. He was never forcible in his approach, but always gently present to lend a helping hand, receiving little to nothing in the way of thanks, for he was, after all, a window.

The only explanation could be that the self-serving of London must have had an open mind to magic, believing that doors held themselves open and items they had lost to the floor found their way back into their clutches miraculously. He may have been Sallow by name, but he was absolutely compassionate by nature.

As time catapulted forward, as it did every bustling Christmas Eve, he bid his final customers the compliments of the season. Just as the last were about to depart, his masterpiece sprang to life once more, its enchanting tune announcing the arrival of midday. This was fortuitous to say the least, as that final customer added two extra pennies to the tin, accompanied by a full-hearted smile.

Sebelius turned the key in the lock to shield himself from those in search of last-minute trinkets. Pausing, a thought flickered across his mind — how would his friend get in? He hesitated and unfastened the door, but he did, however, twirl the sign, changing its stance to 'Closed'.

Fuelled by anticipation and excitement, emotions he seldom experienced, Sebelius found them becoming more familiar since seeing his friend the previous Saturday. He deferred the arrangement of his collar to the judgement of the mirror. The clockmaker, who had never thought himself handsome, was uncharacteristically so. His hands danced through his hair, fingers adjusted his cravat, he smoothed the creases from his jacket, like an artist perfecting his canvas. As a final flourish, he adjusted the sprig of mistletoe and holly in his buttonhole.

Attention now turned to his shop, and Sebelius's diligent hands set about repositioning pieces that curious shoppers had disturbed in their search for an elusive gift. His heart held a special intention: to unveil to Bravington his hideaway, a modest workshop where each element of his craft lay cocooned within a grand wooden chest, each drawer holding the component of his talent — meticulously sorted and alphabetised.

There was a specific place where brushes nestled beside chains, circlips cozied up to cogs, and dials rested alongside springs. Fixings, forgings, and glasses coexisted harmoniously with hairsprings, hands, and keys.

Each component performed its own task. The lines and mainsprings would bridge the gap between potential and movement, while nuts and rivets whispered of those connections yet to be forged. Pendulums were ready to sway with the gravity of time's dance, as the weights that balanced them offered pace within the intricate choreography. Ratchet wheels and ropes waited, in their fashion, to embrace the concept of tension, while washers and wires tiptoed between productivity and space.

Screws. Screws are important, they hold everything together, just as springs breathe life into rhythm. Suspensions offer a promise of a delicate equilibrium, and tapered pins fix aspirations in place, awaiting the moment to spring forth. This all usually concludes with a ding and a dong.

Eager anticipation pulsated noticeably within the horologist by way of his quickening heartbeat. This feeling, long dormant, had been shelved since… school. Yes, school. It was the end of school that marked the beginning of change, a fleeting deliberation whirred briefly through his mind. Poised and ready, he anxiously counted the passing moments, inwardly noting that each ticking second would bring his friend's imminent reappearance at his door.

It was twenty past the hour, and his friend had yet to arrive. The watchmaker remained unruffled; he was confident that his friend would come. To occupy his mind, Sebelius retrieved the tin containing his customers' donations. He tallied the contents on the gleaming glass surface, adding the sum to the week's already generous contributions.

"Eight pounds, fourteen shillings, and sev'npence," he said proudly. "Not a bad effort at all. Ah, let's not forget the three buttons and an Indian rupee."

He thought this to be a respectable sum for only six days, it was a king's ransom for many, and he settled that next year he would start earlier, in order to greatly amplify the additional provisions that these donations afforded the poor and needy. He placed the donations within one of his signature regal blue velvet pouches.

Time elapsed into an almost inconceivable blur, seconds yielding to minutes and the hands moved so minutely that they scarcely appeared to move at all, until they did. The sweet melody of 'London Waits' serenaded the air twice more. With the arrival of two o'clock, Sebelius admitted to himself, with an unexpected sigh, that his friend would not be gracing this special day with his presence. Sebelius had, once more, been forgotten.

III

Sebelius prepared himself to leave, but he lingered and moved with a certain slow deliberateness. Gazing intently through the frost-webbed windowpane, his eyes fixed upon the fleeting shadows that passed by, a flicker of hope attached to each one, ignited by Bravington's proposal of a second visit.

As yearnings stretched into an eternity of waiting, the cold chains of reality began to tighten their grip around Sebelius's heart, he conceded to the truth. Aubrey Bravington was not coming.

His hand delved into the depths of his coat pocket, and, withdrawing the key to the front door, he found, within the crease of his fingers, a solitary sovereign nestled within.

"Buy something wonderful, or keep it, which I suspect you will. May it bring you luck if nothing else, dear sweet Sebelius," he heard Bravington's words play out as clearly as he had spoken them seven days before.

Sebelius became incensed. "You suspect, do you? Much like your anticipation that I would stand here waiting for you, which I am, taking you at your word?" Sebelius's frustration bounced around his empty shop. Hidden behind his composed exterior, the decimation of disappointment burned deep, and pained him as it might anyone.

"Although I do not show my emotions so readily, it does not mean that I do not feel them," he once observed to his father when he was but a small boy, capturing the essence of his often-mechanical behaviour.

Shaking himself of the turmoil that occupied his mind, he resolved to immerse himself fully in the joys of the season. With determined purpose, he placed Bravington's gifted sovereign into the velvet pouch alongside the donations intended for the workhouse. The golden lettering, proudly displaying his shop's insignia, shimmered in the light's gentle glow. Carefully, he pulled the gold drawstrings, securing the pouch, and tying a decisive knot, he looped the thread through his trousers, ensuring its safekeeping, before he ventured out, his heart now lightened with the generosity of the season.

Now he was ready, yet an invisible force halted him in his tracks. Frozen in time, he felt as though something — or rather, someone — had seized him, gripping not just his chest, but the very core where his heart pulsed. A cooling sensation settled upon the spot, then surged like an icy flame, amplifying his paralysis. His eyes widened, and tears that did not come naturally to him, unaccountably bubbled up. Sebelius was not afraid, just inexplicably sad. There was no malevolence, if anything it could be described as a profound sense of love in this enigmatic embrace — a warning, perhaps, or a sign of foresight urging him to stay. Questions cut along suspicions. Should he grant Aubrey Bravington the chance to arrive? As his consciousness whispered his friend's name and private thoughts summoned his flame-haired image, the sensation intensified, compelling Sebelius to remain still. In that silent moment, between the ticking of a second, the feeling dissipated, granting him freedom of movement once more. With its grasp dispelled, he paused a short while and pressed forward, undeterred and unchanged, toward the door.

In his customary routine, Sebelius checked the handle one final time, confirming it was secure. Just as it had been the first time, and as it was now on his seventh attempt, all was fastened. Satisfied, he stepped back into the shifting world around him. Bathed in the soft, radiant glow of the snowy heavens, Ludgate Hill stretched out before him, against the backdrop of a winter wonderland. St. Paul's Cathedral stood as a majestic sentinel, accentuated by the celestial light. The bells rang out, their unexpected peal startled pigeons near and far, their mid-air flurry looked like smuts of burning paper fluttering en masse from the flames of a fire.

Ludgate Hill, a vital thoroughfare, was clogged with an immense stream of trade, flowing in a double current in both directions, as were the pavements, which teemed with the hurried swarm of pedestrians, causing Sebelius to sway gently along the mass of bustling bodies. He walked with purposeful intent, his gaze no longer fixed on the passing shadows that once held his friend's promise; Sebelius's only contemplation centred on the very purpose that united all souls in the vicinity — Christmas.

The air resonated with a racket of joyful clamour, a dulcet blend of hearty laughter, the lilting notes of carollers, and the intoxicating aroma of roasted chestnuts.

Bundled in threadbare coats and woollen scarves, the singers huddled close, their voices intertwining in a passionate celebration. In the passing around of pocket flasks, each sip fortified them against the cold and lubricated their vocal chords, which led them nicely into 'O Come, All Ye Faithful'.

The chestnut vendors tended their fires, sending sweet, sugary aromas swirling through the crisp air — an irresistible lure to passersby. The tantalising scent coaxed coins from cold fingers eager to quiet their hungry stomachs.

The ladies were mesmerised by the hallucinatory blast of colours of the flower sellers, boasting wreaths of holly and winter foliage of pine, tied with ribbons and bedecked with dried fruits, offering the heightened promise of seasonal beauty.

The gentlemen, and not all were that gentle mind you, were in the midst of severe crapulence from the heady cocktail, known commonly as Christmas spirit, which overflowed in tankards, lifting the hearts of revellers in blissful measure. The draymen toiled tirelessly, replenishing the provisions that fuelled this, ensuring that this spring of euphoria remained unceasing.

Sebelius slowed and ambled aimlessly through the teeming streets, unnoticeable in the hurrying crowd of last-minute shoppers engaged in the exchange of commodities for coin. The roads bustled with the clip-clop of traders' carts heavily laden with produce.

Taking a breath, the young man, whose pleasure was derived from this important day, paused. He wanted nothing more than to drink in Christmas until he was invigorated by every last drop.

There was an inexplicable seduction of the Thames tugging at Sebelius's senses. When he had stepped out of his shop, much later than he had anticipated, his intentions had been clear; to turn left and walk the path leading him toward the Clerkenwell Union workhouse. His aim had been to deliver the funds he had collected, with an eagerness to spread joy to those in desperate need of Christmas cheer. Sebelius longed for a festive atmosphere for all, especially the unfortunate inhabitants who dwelt within the workhouse walls, who had not chosen their circumstances. The course of events, however, had taken a different trajectory, for his thinking was unclear and his confused mind was still guided by Bravington's empty words.

He checked his pocket watch, the time was almost quarter to three, and he was now at a disadvantage. Leaving his establishment at midday would have rewarded him with three extra hours. This temporal lead would have granted the matron of the workhouse leave to arrange the delivery of supplementary provisions. Moreover, that additional time could have enriched Sebelius's own enjoyment of his most cherished day.

The snow-brightness lifted, and Sebelius's eyes adjusted to the wondrous transformation where the dank murky waters of the Thames had reshaped itself into a glacial empire. The frozen river was a living canvas upon which the essence of winter had been artfully brushed by Old Mister Winter, a mythical landscape newly conquered by the Crystal Elf, bejewelled with all the gems in the royal collection. The once-flowing waters sat motionless, arrested by the frost's quiet grasp, in a breathtaking spectacle that captured the very heart of the season.

The normally putrid London air was pure and invigoratingly fresh, a thing quite uncommon. He allowed himself to revel in the possibility that the everyday decay had transformed into diamond particles, now scattered far and wide. As far as the eye could see, the river unfolded like a pristine quilt stitched with threads of playful joy and embroidered with laughter and gaiety. The familiar figures of urchins and mudlarks, who scavenged the river's depths for lost treasures, were replaced by a new presence. Children of all ages, young and old, brimming with unrestrained merriment glided, rather clumsily and ungraciously, across the white expanse.

In spirited revelry, the skaters slipped and slid and tumbled, their cheeks flushed with excitement and glowed rosy with cold, holding tightly onto one another's hands to remain upright. Others robustly drifted on sleighs and sledges, carving paths across the battlefield where snowball fights erupted, icy missiles perilously launched in playful vivacity over the fortress walls and impacting enemy targets with a satisfying thud. Reinforcements were called upon by those men crafted of snow, by dreamy imaginations that truly believed their transient creations were gallant knights and soldiers in their master plan to take back the Ice Kingdom.

For Sebelius, Christmas had begun. He had taken in his fill of the snow-covered vistas that London had to offer, and thought to himself that he should walk to Clerkenwell, then home to sit by a roaring fire and listen to the carollers go door to door. Fate had other ideas, however, and the catastrophe that was about to unfold would have tragic consequences that no one could have foreseen.

IV

In the biting hush of a winter's morning, Sebelius Sallow stirred beneath the linen of his all-too-familiar bed, agitated to free himself from beneath the sheets that covered his head. Even before his eyes fluttered open, caught in that natural interval between sleep and wakefulness, he knew the place that surrounded him. The ability to see was non-essential to sense his room ablaze with sunlight, the sun striking his window magnificently. In the darkness of sleep, he could see it piercing through. His nose twitched at the snowy scene he imagined outside, welcoming the crisp scent that now flooded his nostrils. It was the blend of cold air, which clung to the dusty film lining the window pane, accompanied by the faint sweet musk, permeated by the chilly aroma of varnished wood.

Opening his eyes, anticipating the blissful luminosity of morning to grace the contours of his humble bedroom, all around him nothing but darkness whirled. The dense, dark sediment swirled in the deep gloom, where nothing dared to exist. The atmosphere hung oppressively, as if imbued with a life of its own, yet Sebelius experienced an unexpected lightness within.

The amplified silence shattered abruptly as a familiar voice resonated, calling out in the void, "Sebelius!"

"Father?" he shouted into the strangulated inkiness of silhouettes. "Where are you?"

Shadows gracefully pirouetted on the edges of Sebelius's vision, while white sparks heightened the intensity of his unblinking stare. Seeking inner peace amid turmoil, he resorted to a repeated soliloquy, a rambling discourse to soothe inner conflicts of disorientation, despair, dread, panic, and terror. Oblivious to his surroundings, he struggled to navigate the murky depths of his mind, uncovering concealed threats lurking within this ambiguous place.

In a stroke of good fortune, as if his silent prayers had been answered, a flimsy light materialised, casting an insipid glimmer that caused the darkness to transform, shimmering into wisps of indigo and violet that gradually converged into vibrant blues and greens, unveiling recognisable surroundings that slowly became distinctly clear.

In a means to summon him, Sebelius's name resonated sweetly again.

"Father? I cannot see you!" he shouted. "I cannot see anything," he muttered despondently.

Sebelius was home. He sat up in what he believed was the safety of his bed, surrounded by the familiar — familiar was good, marvellous even — a place eternally known to him. However, profound disappointment engulfed the horologist as his vision faltered under the blinding brilliance of snow. The thought of home ceased to offer solace, it was a trick of luminescence, he was surrounded instead by a desolate expanse of snow and ice. The Thames stretched out, barren and devoid of life. Untouched snow blanketed the landscape, erasing any traces of the joy it once brought. This is where he sat, alone amidst the wintry silence, engulfed with a profound sense of yearning. The young man longed not only for the father, who had loved and comforted him since birth, but for the embrace of the mother, who had passed away when he was on the cusp of conscious memory.

"Father, what is the hour?" In frantic panic he patted his torso for his pocket watch only to feel the fabric beneath his anxious palms — no pocket watch to be found. "Father, I cannot see you!" he protested.

"As I never left you, I am simply here," Enoch Sallow voiced beside him. For the first time in perpetuity, Sebelius's gaze met the glistening iron-blue eyes of his father, and the weight of eight months crashed down. Those moments without his father stretched into days, minutes unfolded like weeks, and hours swept by, bypassing months and years to feel like a lifetime — a lifetime that seemed as if it were only yesterday.

"Father! Is it you?" Sebelius exclaimed with joy, but also great alarm. "Is it truly you?" came the question again with cautious restraint, as if he could hardly bear to hear the answer.

"It is indeed, Sebelius," his father's heartening voice reassured, its gentle intonations tenderly calming the agitation of surprise and bewilderment. "Compose yourself, my son. Worry and upset serves no purpose," he advised, attuned to his son's turmoil.

Enoch Sallow knew that emotions waged war within Sebelius's heart, as he strived to comprehend those feelings that battled and raged, surging more intensely than he was accustomed to. The conflict of intense passion and loss sought release, yet he had all the patience of a tree — always feeling but never showing.

In a rush of jubilant joy, Sebelius threw himself forward with his arms clasping tightly around his father, as he did when he fumbled into his bedroom on that fateful afternoon, finding Enoch writhing in contorted agony upon the floor. His incomprehensible screams substantiated to no real cause, save that he hurt all over. Racing eighteen doors down to summon the doctor, Sebelius returned within moments, the physician trailing behind. But by then, it was too late. Enoch Sallow had slipped away, the pressure within causing an internal rupture to burst like a dammed river, flooding his body with the very fluid that gave life. His son cradled his father's lifeless body, the warmth fading, as he prayed for his own death.

Gently pressing his cheek to his father's shoulder, Sebelius gripped him tightly. The forearms that crossed his back radiated a warmth born of the love cultivated during every second of absence.

"I have missed you like a timepiece ticking along without hands," Sebelius said, drawing in the comforting scent of his father's shirt, the sweet soapy perfume of his skin, and the musk of Macassar lingering in his hair. He smelled the same as he always had. He was real, and their reunion was all that mattered; the how, why, or wherefores were of no consequence.

"Come now, you must prepare yourself!" Enoch Sallow commanded gently.

"Where have you been? Why did you leave me?" He mournfully pulled his father even tighter.

"Come, come, Sebelius, I never left you. I have been right by your side whenever you needed me," he retorted gently.

"There have been so many times I've paused in readiness to share news or seek your guidance, and you have not been there," Sebelius whispered.

"And did you not speak those things to me in your mind?"

"Yes, and more often than not, out loud," he said indignantly.

"I was there… listening. Although I might not have had the ability to respond, I listened… and you were never alone."

The young man gently gripped his father by the shoulders, holding him at arm's length, too afraid to let him go as if he might lose him all over again. "There have been so many questions that required a solution, and—" he paused.

"Did the answer not come to you?"

"Yes, but I needed you!"

"I spoke the answers to you and you claimed the solutions as your own," Enoch said and smiled, causing his moustache to spread higher across his handsome face, the skin wrinkling around the eyes and peeking behind the frames of his spectacles. "It is how it should be."

"I thought I should die without you," Sebelius admitted. "I prayed for it."

"And did you?" his father asked.

"No."

"That is because it was not your time."

"Neither was it yours!"

"I'm sorry to say, it was."

"No, we made plans." Sebelius scolded his father defiantly. "You and I, you always said—"

"I was awfully tired, and I was called to rest."

"You never said," Sebelius refuted emotionally. "You could have said. I would have done more."

"I didn't know it myself," his father declared tenderly. "It was only when I closed my eyes that I found I desperately needed it. You did all you could, you never left my side, and moreover you were my only reason for living. You have been the only reason I continue along the mortal coils of life, unseen, because you are in it."

"I have shed so many tears for you, unseen," Sebelius confessed. "My heart broke, and until today, it has never truly healed."

"I have acknowledged every tear and felt the burden of your heartbreak," Enoch recognised.

"Has my grief disturbed your peace in the afterlife?"

"No, you foolish thing. The afterlife allows us to carry the impediments we knew in life unburdened. Your tears have brought me unhappiness, and your heartache has brought me the same deal of sorrow, but it does not impede me. I grow stronger as a result of your love. The most damaging thing that can happen to a spirit is to be forgotten, and to lack a sense of purpose."

"Are there many forgotten spirits?"

"There are countless, I'm sad to say," replied Enoch Sallow. The expression on his son's face prompted him to elaborate. "Consider all those who have ever been born, or those who nearly existed. Each possesses a soul. It's family and lineage that carry us forward when our mortal selves cease to exist. We are woven into stories to be passed down through generations, immortalised in art and its many forms. We hope that we've done enough, lived enough, loved enough, been good enough — or for some, bad enough — all to be remembered. So yes, the number of forgotten spirits outweighs those remembered, but there are those living today who are already forgotten, and yet they still breathe. Your love has kept this weary old spirit strong."

"Honestly?" Sebelius asked sadly.

"Honestly," Enoch attested. "You have always made me

stronger, but, with time, tears transform into smiles, pain into laughter, and grief, ever-present as second nature, becomes the driving force for carrying on."

Sebelius's heart lifted with the appreciation that he was once more with his beloved papa.

"Father?"

"Yes, my son?" he answered inquisitively.

"Why do you visit me... now?"

His father — the man who tenderly cradled him through sickness, swiftly responded to his every call, imparted invaluable lessons at every turn, and steadfastly stood by his side, guiding him to face life's adversities head-on when the world seemed to turn its back — stared into the breach of having to soothe one more cruelty.

"Where is Mother?" Sebelius inquired.

Perhaps two more cruelties. Enoch's eyes sought refuge in the glistening snow.

"Are you reunited?" Sebelius pressed.

"Not exactly," his father admitted.

"What *exactly* does that mean?" Sebelius pleaded anxiously. "Why is she not with you?"

This brought forth a broken repertoire, constructed of utterances of what seemed to be an excuse created without forethought or substance.

"Father, you said that when we die, the ones we love the most are there, at that pivotal moment, to guide us into the next life, and there we shall be together, forever. Where is Mother?"

"It is true, Sebelius. I never... what I mean to say is... all will become clear. Things might seem hazy now, but you will learn everything that has ever been, and all that is yet to come will be known to you. In the beginning, the periphery of the world, between the living and those passed, can be tenuous, and parallels blur, causing the particles of memory to fragment and rebuild in your afterlife."

"Remember what? Father, where is my mother?" Sebelius demanded with remonstrated force. "She should have been with you to ease your passing. I wish to see her!"

Enoch began to interject.

"I demand to see her!" Sebelius exclaimed disapprovingly.

"I never lied about the souls of our loved ones reuniting in death. I have proved it, as I do now." Enoch said penitently. "I will show you, and you will remember. It won't be easy, but, as it is in life, our deliverance to acceptance comes through the trials of the pain."

V

Through the air, snowballs were hurtling at the heads of unsuspecting targets. Away from the battlefield a rumour was tossed around to cause great delight, and this crystallised into a more definite shape as eyes confirmed what ears had heard — Queen Victoria herself, yet uncrowned, and on her first Christmas, was making her grand journey from London to Windsor along the banks of the Thames in her horse-drawn carriage. Euphoric at the prospect of witnessing such an occasion, a rush of anticipation erupted through the throng on the ice that settled upon the river. In a chorus of undivided enthusiasm, explosive hollers and jubilant cheers, the thrill-seekers hastily abandoned the frozen expanse, like a herd of stampeding beasts on the barren plains of Africa.

Standing with his father, Sebelius watched on as the mass of eager onlookers swelled.

"There you are," his father said, tugging at his arms and pointing. Sebelius caught sight of himself amidst the horde, thrust suddenly and unwillingly into the gleeful anticipation at the sight of the new queen. As he observed himself, Sebelius witnessed the rush of angst on his own face, remembering the fear of the clambering and shoving of the crowd. Crowds caused him immense dread. Their voices garbled and cackled nonsense, spewing out tales of past royal processions, while others commented on the young lady's radiance.

He gingerly slipped his hand into his trouser pocket, pressing his knuckles against the velvet pouch with its strings still tied securely, wary of surrendering the generous offerings to the opportunistic pickpockets and vagabonds who were known to exploit such situations to their full advantage.

"The money? Where is the money?" he shouted, looking on. "I had it there. I had it still."

"Shhh. Patience, Sebelius." His father mollified him with a touch of his hand.

The young Queen, aware of the immense public interest in her journey, signalled early on to her coachman for the speed to be reduced to a gentle canter. With grace and regal poise, she waved a delicate hand and paid her heartfelt reverence to her adoring subjects. The length of those gathered rang out with fervent cheers.

On the Thames, panic began with a ripple, spreading swiftly among the crowds. It escalated into a destructive deluge as the brittle surface beneath the feet of the skaters started to creak and groan. Anxious legs lunged forward, their blades biting into the ice as they sprang toward the bank, causing fractures to emerge and exposing intricate weakened patterns across the frozen expanse. A banded shriek rose up from those on the ice, while those on the embankment remained oblivious; with their backs to the Thames, their attention fixed, their own cheers drowned out any rumblings of danger. Yet the revellers scrambled and hurled themselves toward the safety of land, their happiness spent, and now held to ransom by a rising tide of fear.

"Stay calm!" bellowed a voice carrying above the din of chaos.

But calm was easier said than done, as the surface continued to fragment with an ominous symphony of snaps and groans. Those seekers of excitement, who frantically abandoned their skates, clamoured in a desperate rush, their feet pounding against the glacial fragments in a frantic bid to save themselves. The once-festive, celebratory scene, reminiscent of any Christmas romanticism that all strive to re-create, had hurtled into a vision of pandemonium. Each crying voice belonged to someone trying to escape the peril of death.

Having come to the end of the line of adoring spectators, the royal coachman engaged the usual velocity and the source of everyone's entertainment now faded quickly into the distance. Hearts and faces glowed, yet their delight dimmed under the shadow of danger gripping their present reality as spectators witnessed chaos on the Thames. Shrieks and strained cries mingled with the sound of cracking ice.

A call for unity rang out. Strangers tore branches off trees and others linked arms to assist one another, but the urgency of the rescue demanded greater determination, turning their efforts into an anguished struggle to form a human chain to bridge the perilous gap between solid ground and the bitter, icy terrain. The links strained under the pressure as desperation gripped them like the aching fingers that tightly clutched and tore at fabric, reaching out desperately for the welcoming arms extended to rescue them.

Teetering on the edge, Sebelius was quick to play his part, his eyes fixed on a small boy who had snuck away from his family and was now alone. The watchmaker found himself fused to the spot, fear tightening its grip while his mind raced through frantic calculations to determine the best course of action. His consciousness snapped back into focus when his ears were pierced by a heart-wrenching cry from the endangered lad, who could not have been more than two years of age. The boy's eyes widened with terror, and his flailing little form suddenly vanished beneath the ice's treacherous veneer.

Springing into action, in a measured cadence and setting his mind to focus, words flowed from Sebelius's lips, a rhythm to quell his fear.

"Silent night, holy night, all is calm, all is bright. Round yon virgin, mother and child, holy infant so tender and mild." He emphasised each word as if orchestrating a melody to quieten his thoughts and still his anxious heart. "Sleep in heavenly peace, sleep in heavenly—"

Before his tossed coat could land on the icy bank, Sebelius bravely, albeit clumsily, plunged himself into the waters. As his last strand of hair was submerged, a hundred thousand million ice-cold needles blitzed his face, inflicting the torment of excruciating misery that caused every nerve in his head to pulsate. Every fibre beneath his skin seemed to crystallise and intertwine, forming a substantial tangled knotted mass. Then, at the peak of agony, the anguish erupted from his head, though on the verge of exploding and escalated to every part of his body.

"I'm going to die," Sebelius said to himself, and that became the final coherent thought he was likely to have as everything began to freeze. He could never have envisaged that the first thing to freeze in frigid waters was the capacity to think.

Blinking hard at the lifeless form of the child who was clenched by the frigid hand of death, Sebelius regained his composure and, with a determined thrash of his arms, he broke free from the despondency of impending doom. He wallowed through the thick waters to reach the child. His numbing fingers, requiring great effort, clamped the shoulders of the small frame.

Pulling the boy into his chest, Sebelius kicked his legs to propel himself to the surface, exhaling all at once in a hope of making himself lighter.

"My boy!" roared the voice of the child's father. He stood as a slender figure, his shoulders resembling two beanpoles, each topped with an egg, and his coat bundled over them. His head was elongated, and his face kind and intelligent. A top hat passed down by a few hands, ill-fitted and too large for his head, sat with accustomed heaviness on his ears. The red tint of cold on his nose and cheeks transformed into a florid blaze of gut-wrenching panic at the sight of his small boy in danger. Clad in a tarnished black frock-coat, fastened at the front with the collar upturned, and a muffler bubbling up to his chin, he urgently waved his scrawny arms to summon help for his child. The wrists of this poor figure protruded from straggly sleeves, devoid of cuffs or a visible shirt.

He swiftly tore the child from Sebelius's barely visible grasp as soon as the tiny child was seen, and he in turn handed him to the safety of those attending to the casualties.

"My little, little child!" his father cried. "My little child!"

In blind panic, Sebelius exploded to his father as he watched his living self lose the battle, "I have to help... I have to help me!"

Enoch placed his hand on his son's chest. "Stop, please, there is nothing you can do. Sebelius—" but he broke free and hastened full pelt across the snow towards himself. His father raised his hand from the spot where he stood, bringing his son to an abrupt halt.

"Father, let me go. Release me so that I might save myself!"

"Sebelius, no! I couldn't help you then, and you can't help yourself now. There's nothing you can do."

Clinging to the edge, exhausted and mostly swallowed by the freezing water, Sebelius tried to call out, yearning to be pulled to safety and warmed, but the uncontrollable shiver rendered any speech futile.

For an instant, Sebelius closed his eyes and was roused to a conscious mind by the weighty tug at his waist from beneath the water. In his delirium, a split-second thought brought to mind the young boy that was drowning, pulling at him to be saved, but relief came in seeing that the child was in the safest of hands on the snowy bank. The tugging beneath came from the velvet sack containing the eight pounds, fourteen shillings, and seven pence — not forgetting the gold sovereign.

Panic recoiled at the recollection that there was one more demand upon his time, to deliver the money to the Union workhouse. As despair overran, a fleeting peace settled over him, recalling a snippet once heard, or read, that drowning was not a difficult death; among all methods, it was considered the most painless and certainly preferable. Sebelius concluded it was a lie. It was not without pain, for he endured excruciating agony.

In the continued horror of the bringing of others to safety, a tree branch was thrust into the water, and it was against this that Sebelius secured himself as he wrestled the murky waters. Submerging his head beneath the water in an attempt to free the pouch, his weakness caused him to descend once more into the depths. The deplorable cold and the pesky string which secured the pouch made his attempts appear futile. His fingers fumbled with the cord to free the money and allow it to find a safe space upon the surface, hoping to be rescued next.

Writhing beneath the booming furore, the sky's brightness flashed with anarchy above, the cold stripping a lifetime of comfort from his soul. Blood congealed into slush, flesh pierced by gelid skewers, lungs ablaze through breathless ransom. At the point of death, one never feels so alive.

From the depths of hysteria, his mind hummed a familiar tune, and inwardly he spoke the words, "Silent night, holy night, all is calm, all is bright—," its melody accompanying him, so he did not feel so alone. Its soothing notes, his only solace, persisted until another figure emerged — Aubrey Bravington. A fire of auburn hair swaying in the icy water, a beautiful smile framed by a perfectly trimmed flame-like beard, and a gaze that locked with Sebelius's, a fleeting moment feeling like a lifetime in the intensity of expiration.

Above, on the icy plain, his anguished spirit screamed and bellowed, urging the dying man to hold on, and pleading with him to fight against the cold and summon the strength to stay alive.

In his empty shop, the grand timepiece that hung upon the chimney breast, bearing the heart and soul of its creator, resonated with the chime of three. The robust toll of 'London Waits' echoed, while other timepieces in the assembly remained uncharacteristically silent at this hour.

It was three o'clock.

"Help him, please! Please, help him! Help me!" Sebelius appealed to swarms of mortal bodies caught in the pandemonium, but he was invisible to all. "Please, my lady, over there. He needs help!" he beseeched. "Please, sir! Please, help!" Sebelius implored one man who scurried by, and who, as if somehow sensitive to the pleading spirit's presence, came to a sudden stop.

At first glance he might have been a gentleman, with steely grey eyes, and whose step fell heavy upon the snow. He observantly studied the faces of casualties receiving aid. From under wild, grey thorny brows, he surveyed each face in turn, hoping to recognise someone. His countenance revealed no concern for the welfare of a lost loved one.

Enormous fear and dislike struck those who caught sight of him. His raw-boned, withered frame exuded a vast submission to greed, yet his wealth failed to nourish his body or soul. His face, cold and hard as if sculpted from marble, lacked colour and smoothness. Cruel and unfeeling, it bore deep lines etched into every possible space — a disfigurement of every unkindness, each dreadful deed a hammer-strike against the chisel that bore those wrinkle lines.

Once a young gentleman of the City, gentleness had long abandoned its place among his limited attributes. Now an unscrupulous moneylender, he sought out his debtors to calculate potential losses. The icy stares and glares around him hinted that almost all present either owed him money currently or had in the past.

"Sir, I implore you, please help! I'm over there!" Sebelius roared at the unflinching man as his father looked on, heartbroken. The man paused and glanced around calmly in the frenzied maelstrom of dismay. Could Sebelius be heard?

In his natural spindly stride, devoid of urgency, he moved towards the place where Sebelius floundered. He seized the horologist by the scruff of his suit jacket, which puffed at the neck where water and air had become trapped.

"Thank you, sir! A million times, I thank you!" Sebelius thanked the man, freeing himself from his father's grasp and dashing forward to reunite with his former self.

"Sebelius, no!" Enoch blasted, raising his hand again, bringing his son to an immediate halt.

"Father, please. I don't want him to be alone!"

The moneylender fought and dragged Sebelius onto the ice. Perished to the bone. He was as rigid as if carved from wood. His lips were taut, yet held every intention to impart sincere gratitude and provide precise instructions for depositing the money. His eyes, wide with a fleeting sparkle, held onto that glimmer for only a few seconds more before it dissolved into a solitary tear. Like a clock in need of winding, he ceased to tick any more.

Sebelius's lifeless form was soon laid on the bank. The metallic sound of rubbing coins resonated as the pouch still clutched within his frozen fingers, found its place to rest beside him on the snow.

The man, whose fancy it had been to call himself a gentleman, was merely a lurcher in fine threads. On hearing the tinkling sound, he responded with a broad, glistening stare. This prompted the bristly bushes above his eyes to take flight upon his forehead, and the lines etched in his brow to deepen even further. Money and all its sounds were as familiar to him as flowers to a countryman. As he scrutinised Sebelius's face, he could not place him. A sense of reassurance washed over him. This man, he concluded, was not leaving this world with any debts unsettled, not now, nor had Sebelius ever been an unfortunate debtor to this man.

He extracted the pouch from Sebelius's icy grasp and pocketed the money, after ensuring that he was not being observed. After all, what use is money to a man who breathes no longer?

"Over there," the thieving scoundrel said to a rescuer, tilting his head toward the spot where Sebelius lay. His words were uttered with little to no significance.

Sebelius Sallow lay lifeless, and both he and his father gazed on in solemn silence.

VI

At last it was over.

Those who had been rescued found solace and warmth, while the injured were recovering in the comforting embrace of charity. Out of the countless thousands of revellers, it is estimated that more than five hundred fell victim to the frigid waters, with a little over two hundred of those sustaining injuries, including broken bones, cuts, and bruises. Ninety-eight perished, as the body count would corroborate. Who knows how many more souls lingered, unnoticed, unmourned, and undiscovered on the riverbed, destined for eternity?

The lifeless bodies of those who, only a short moment ago, laughed and played, their lips ringing out the words of "Merry Christmas" and "Season's Greetings", were arranged in rows on the snowy bank like fish carefully arrayed in a fishmonger's window, their faces veiled with calico rags.

Policemen knelt at the head of each victim, lifting the plain-woven scraps to unveil their faces to potential loved ones. Standing at their feet, they harboured a double hope — one of relief that it was their kin spared from death, allowing hope to prevail, and the other that their beloved's body had been rescued from the watery abyss of the Thames and could be laid to rest.

Oh, the closure a funeral bestows, each step toward the journey's end offers acceptance and peace for both the living and the departed. Oh, how we yearn for a tranquil resting place, a sunny spot where the warmth of summer lingers and a frosty winter sky stands frozen in time. If possible, a modest little stone inscribed with our name, not to recount achievements or wrongdoings but to gently remind the bustling world, as it inexorably marches forward, that this soul embraced life within the sacred span from the hallowed year of birth to the sorrowful year of demise. It becomes a sanctuary for repose, a destination for the solace of loved ones, and a poignant marker heralding the commencement of a new, poorer existence for those who remain.

"The Thames would be an awful grave to visit," murmured one of the police constables beneath his moustache to his colleague, rhythmically beating his hands against his caped chest and uniformed thighs to stave off the biting cold.

"That it would," came the grim reply, as both fell silent and dropped to their knees to display the faces of those in their charge.

The fortunate shook their heads, tears streaming down their faces, while the less fortunate sobbed uncontrollably into their gloves or sank to the ground. The once-vibrant skirts and coats, which had danced freely in the Christmas merriment, lay heavy on the ice and snow. Now, deprived of their original purpose to provide warmth to those lost, they were saturated and rigid, the cold transforming water into ice particles within the fabrics' fibres.

The spirits of those departed stood, knelt, or sat beside their mortal remains, quite dumbfounded, observing the relatives of others gazing at their lifeless forms, shedding tears for the sorrowful loss. They swallowed down their gratitude that the faces did not belong to their own family. One by one, the bodies were claimed, until only a few remained, and dusk began to set in.

"He left me," Sebelius muttered with incredulity. "I cannot believe that he took the money and left me. I don't see how you showing me this has helped!"

"Each spirit must make peace with how they met their end. The events of your demise would come back in time, but the sooner acceptance is sought, the easier it is to move on. This is where I found you," Enoch Sallow said mournfully, standing behind his son, who sat in the snow and at the right shoulder of his mortal being.

"You talk of acceptance? I shall never accept this which has befallen me. What wrongs have I committed?"

"None. You have committed none, on the contrary, great things await you, Sebelius, all this has happened for a reason," his father said encouragingly.

"I will never believe that my life was cut so short, because of what, some greater purpose? No, I do not believe that. Despite the unremarkable nature of my existence, and the scant impact I made, I still had enough purpose to continue living, to create some semblance of meaning..." In his hysteria, Sebelius erupted into laughter. "Who am I trying to deceive? I've never made a difference. Today, I saved a child's life, yet the father hardly acknowledged me —"

"What you did was brave and selfless—"

"It was irrational and foolhardy. The greatest climax of the joke, when help does materialise, the allure of money outweighs any significance I might have had. Trust me, Father, there is no grand purpose."

"Trust me when I say, it is your time."

"And what is my reason? Was I tired too? Because I wasn't and I'm not."

There was a profound silence.

Beside him, a larger piece of calico veiling a small frame began to stir. Sebelius exchanged glances with his father as he knelt beside the stirring form and attempted to lift the cloth, but his hand passed through. He took a hard gulp, appreciating for the first time that, although he seemed to inhabit the world as he always had, he had no power to effect real action.

Enoch Sallow raised his hand before him, and the shroud folded away as gently as a feather in a breeze. What Sebelius saw was not what he was expecting. On the snow lay the body of a young child, of five or six, her flaxen hair limp upon the soft, white cushioned ground. Her thin, cold, blue lips were slightly parted, revealing an imperfect row of discoloured teeth, but she remained an angelic little urchin. Nestled beside the lifeless body, another small child, identical in appearance, with scrawny arms wrapped around the insufficient neck wore the exact same ragged dress, a white tattered comforter, and inadequate boots.

"Hello, little one," Sebelius said, capturing the girl's attention. She untucked her face from the nook of the little neck she hugged tightly, revealing sad eyes, then hid her face again in the same spot.

He placed his hand on her tiny shoulder, kneeling beside the child in a bid to rouse her. "Little one," he said, giving her the gentlest of reassuring shakes. "You are safe," he reassured her.

"Go away," the childish voice said reproachfully. "I want to get back in," she said, pushing her spirit form as close to her remains as possible, hoping to cross the bridge back to human existence.

Feeling the weight of her pain of suffering, Sebelius paused.

"I must get back in. I must find Mother," the child said with a solemnity that was heightened by the slushy, raspy sound of her lateral lisp. "Please help me find her."

He looked up at his father, "What are we to do?"

"There isn't anything we can do," Enoch Sallow said helplessly.

"We can't leave her, Father. If this child were me and I were alone, you would want someone to help me."

"The laws and principles of life are not the same as those in death. A loved one will come shortly, a sudden demise of human life can delay the greeting by a loved one," his father clarified.

"Where is her mother?" Sebelius supplicated, his gaze darting back and forth between his father and the tragic child.

"If she perished then they will be reunited soon, and if she survived, the mention of the child's name, or even a fleeting thought will summon this little one's spirit to her."

Enoch was forced to elaborate upon a law of the spirit world, prompted by his son's questioning look. "When a spirit vacates the human body, they are met by the loved ones of those whose hearts overflowed with love in life. The transition is easy and painless, a spiritual crescendo to that great symphony of existence. Many who pass suddenly or without warning may take a little longer to find."

"I have so many questions." Sebelius paused and plucked the first that came to him. "You said she would be summoned at the mere mention of her name?"

"Soon after death, a spirit usually remains with their loved ones left behind, until they are laid to rest. Hence why it is indicated that the presence of the recently departed can still be felt," Enoch presented.

"I knew you were with me!" Sebelius exclaimed passionately, his suspicions confirmed. "I could feel you."

"I seldom left your side to begin with, but as time went on and you became more resolute in your grief, I did leave you. But when you thought of me or spoke about me, it pulled me immediately back to you."

"So, when this little one's mother thinks of her or mentions her name, she will be drawn immediately to her?," added Sebelius.

"Absolutely, or anyone who loves her," his father said assuredly.

"Did you hear that, little one?" Sebelius said excitedly, giving her a gentle shake at her shoulder. "We will get you back to your mother."

"Please let me be. I just wish to live so I can see my mother," she said determinedly, without lifting her head from the nook where her head was buried.

"Would you, at the very least, look at me, little one?" Sebelius asked, his expression pained.

"No, thank you. Let me be, please. I shall stay here, and she will look for me," the girl sobbed. "She has to find me."

"That told you," his father observed with a concealed smile. "She is nothing but polite, even when giving you your marching orders."

"Well, I shan't leave you be," Sebelius declared obstinately. He settled down, backside first, tucking his legs into himself until his knees touched his chin. "When you are ready to be my friend, let me know."

The elder Mr Sallow couldn't help but offer an inquisitive smile, marvelling at the transformation of his socially awkward, intensely focused, literal and laterally thinking, routine-abiding son. In this moment of emotional turbulence, something he often found challenging, Sebelius proved he could be more of a petulant child than... a petulant child.

"Won't you tell me your name, little one?" Sebelius asked.

"Adelaide," she mumbled reluctantly with her head still burrowed.

"I'm very pleased to meet you, Adelaide. I'm Sebelius Sallow, and this is my father, Enoch."

Despite her unkempt appearance of scant clothes, which, by anyone's guess, had seen a few previous hands, the child may have lacked the comfort of wealth, but clearly not the love of a mother. If love were the true currency of life, she would be among the wealthiest, possessing boundless riches beyond measure.

"How do you do?" Adelaide responded, lifting her head a little further away from the comfort of her embrace.

"I promise you, Adelaide... whatever your surname might be—"

"Brindle," she interjected.

"Very well. Brindle. I promise you, Adelaide Brindle, that we shall get you back to your blessed mother before Christmas is through."

"You promise, Mr Sallow?" she spoke excitedly, her words sounding watery and indistinct.

"I said so, didn't I?" he said, exchanging an amused glance with his father.

Adelaide Brindle leaped from the side of her former self and threw herself around Sebelius's neck, making him start. Although unaccustomed to feeling the joys of physical friendliness, he could sense that he was not only transitioning from one universe into another, but he himself into a person he might have hoped to be when he inhabited his vessel of flesh and bone.

"Mother calls me Laidey," she said coyly.

"I am very pleased to meet you, Laidey," Enoch said, taking her hand and giving a careful bow.

"As am I, little Laidey," Sebelius concluded.

"Over 'ere, guv!" thundered the voice of a man carrying a lamp, who was followed by two strong horses pulling a large open-top cart, topped with a driver. The mighty wheels crunched against the snow, compacting it into a ribbon beneath. Either side of the cart, there was an escort of tall, thickset men, in black weeds, top hat and heavy matching frock coats, with mufflers pulled up to their noses.

"There's two more 'ere," the same voice instructed, gliding his torch above the remains of Sebelius and Laidey. "The poor souls, these are the last two unclaimed."

The two gentlemen, clad all in black, who chaperoned each side of the cart, stood top and tail, towering over Sebelius's body. The carriage driver turned the coach around in a full circle, so they could load on those others who were unclaimed.

The horses trotted dejectedly in the direction towards Sebelius, Enoch, and Laidey. Unaware that their existence was merely a shadow of their past selves and mortal dangers could no longer harm them, Laidey flung herself in front of her companions with arms spread wide to protect them. This caused the mighty beasts to pause and rear up.

"Move on!" called the driver above his muffler, somewhat perturbed at this unexplained reaction, for these creatures never behaved out of turn. They made an attempt at a bow of their heads and froze, staring stoically ahead.

The three spirits stepped aside to clear a path for the carriage to pass, and as they did so, both creatures emitted a mighty snort and snarl, their breath forming clouds in the air before them. This signalled to the driver that they were now ready to proceed. Sebelius's remains were then loaded onto the wagon, with Laidey placed close beside him, totalling thirteen occupants, their destination the undertaker's warehouse.

With no reason to linger, the three trailed behind the cart, only to discover they weren't alone. These mortal remains, uncollected in death, mirrored the unclaimed souls that traversed alongside them. These forgotten entities mourned their own loss, as there was no one else to do it on their behalf.

VII

Darkness fell; creeping around corners, peeping through door locks, whispering down chimneys, and pushing itself through window panes to fill every available space. When doors opened and closed, it was the same darkness that stood on either side; it was everywhere. There is nothing so thoroughly foreboding as darkness when in the midst of sorrow. It was this darkness that called to the lamp carriers, each touched by the tragedy either personally or through sympathy, to a poignant vigil that night. Carols resonated across the Thames, breaking the deathly stillness of oppressive grief with the message of rejoicing birth, welcoming light and the spirit of giving, reminding all of the importance of kindness, compassion, joy, hope, and, most importantly, love.

"I feel him close to me," wept a middle-aged woman into her sodden handkerchief. She couldn't have been more correct, the spirit of her dearly departed son clung to her arm, pleading for her not to grieve so bitterly, as her sorrow unsettled him. Sebelius could only look on, feeling as helpless as when the ice first gave way.

A mass of souls gathered on the embankment, drifting in the air above and settling on the remnants of the frozen ice plain. Ethereal loved ones welcomed the departed, facilitating a seamless transition into the new life, as Enoch had done for his son.

Those who remained and grieved, through mention or mere thought of their nearest and dearest, drew them close. Helpless spirits could only watch, unable to ease the immeasurable pain of those suffering.

"Who, pray tell, is he?" Sebelius asked his father aghast.

"Hush. Lower your tone," his father rebuked.

Sebelius spoke of a wraithlike silhouette, a gigantic, brawny figure clad in a coarse hessian hooded cloak, crudely trimmed with the furs of long-deceased creatures. Laidey marvelled, as any child does at anything out of the ordinary, not foreseeing any possible menace, untarnished by the learned prejudices of other people's influence.

"In life, he was Einar Hawksbane, a Viking warrior," Enoch Sallow whispered. "He was feared by all, and so complacent was he in his reputation his lands were ransacked and pillaged, just as he had acquired them from rival factions. Now he spiritually embodies a greater rule."

Einar's immense bulk propelled him forward with deliberate force, swaying from left to right in a rhythmic motion, effortlessly carrying the burden of perpetual languor, immune to punctuality. His languid form ambled amidst the unclaimed souls, murmuring ambiguous chants from beneath the swath of chestnut hair flowing from his face, fashioned in a myriad of intricate plaits and braids and fastened periodically with golden rings.

"Strength summoned from the depths within, with a resilient heart, healing shall begin," echoed the Viking's words that caught Sebelius's ear.

The ghostly denizens, trailing beside their loved ones, remained silent.

"Well?" Sebelius whispered. "What greater ordinance?"

"Sloth," Enoch discreetly named him.

"Sloth?" Sebelius repeated, the alarm taking his tone several octaves higher.

At the shrill mention of his name, Einar pointed heavy-lidded eyes in their direction, followed by a grunt of annoyance at the mention of his presence. His countenance unmistakably portrayed a warrior in every sense. So impressive was this colossus that it elicited an audible gasp from Laidey.

"Sloth? The deadly sin, Sloth?" Sebelius said in a more amenable tone.

"Shush, Sebelius. Yes, the very same" his father scolded.

It became evident why he could strike fear when presented as the opposition in war. His large head, a solid lump of bone encased in Nordic weathered skin, draped with the chestnut glow of hair to match the already mentioned beard. Each battle and conquest had left its mark against the contours of his manly face, radiating a clear warning that he was not to be trifled with.

"In the storm of death, a resilient tide gives birth to strength where shadows subside," spoke Sloth, the ambassador of denial, in a deep, heavy-laboured tone. "By working through, shock and denial cease. It is only then you will find true peace," the warrior concluded, ambling along slowly, when the unfortunate spirit of a woman, who perished in the tragedy, grasped the Viking ruler by his fur trim, and they both vanished.

"Confusion might be commonplace when, oh, I don't know, you transition from the realm of the living to that of eternal life. But, I welcome you to intervene at any juncture and explain to me why the deadly sin of Sloth is interfering with the recently deceased." Sebelius said caustically. "And, why did he disappear with that spirit?"

"Your newfound assertiveness is leaving you rather bumptious. Cut it out, it is beneath you, Sebelius Sallow," his father scolded, silently questioning how much of his own living-self had altered since his transition into death.

Enoch elaborated on how the initial shock and disbelief in the first stage of grief, often leading to insensibility and avoidance, impacts not only those left behind but the newly departed. Touching the cloak of an appointed spirit signifies consent, allowing them to guide a lost soul fully into the transition of the next stage of acceptance.

His son appeared unconvinced.

"Living in this parallel realm can feel as if we exist behind glass, walking freely among those we love and observe, yet we ourselves go unnoticed. Upon their mortal departure and subsequent arrival into the ever after, seven beings were chosen, by their actions in life, to become the spirits that represent the seven deadly sins, tasked to aid and be of use in death. They shape the actions of the living and aid the understanding of those among the departed, you see?"

"Why, no. I don't," Sebelius confessed doggedly. "In whose infinite wisdom came the idea that Sloth should be the stimulus to overcome any stage of grief?"

"Sebelius Sallow, He and He alone," Enoch announced, naming the deity. "Sloth is the perfect pairing, as the first stage of grief marks a disengagement with reality, and that reluctance is no better seen than in Sloth."

"It's all too bizarre," Sebelius acknowledged incredulously.

"You will find it even more so when you discover that the Sins are wed to the Virtues."

"Well, of course. Why wouldn't they be?"

"In order to mend what is broken, the Deadly Sin, that is Sloth, as Einar is aptly named, is not only assigned to its appropriate stage of grief but he is paired in this realm with Diligence. Through her virtue, Sloth becomes a greater advocate, exhorting the courage, faith, hope, and steadfastness needed to grow strong," Enoch presented. "And there she stands," he observed, as they beheld before them a vision of pure femininity and strength; a lady of African descent, adorned in her native attire, rich and sumptuous, emblazoned with the shapes and patterns inspired by her ancestral heritage. Iridescent gold threads traced every element of the design, imbuing the fabric with the rich warmth and cultural heart of Africa.

"She is beautiful," Laidey asserted soothingly, referring specifically to the exotic gown that fitted every contour of her shape and the headdress of swirling fabrics that sat framing her angelic face.

"She is a potent antidote to her husband," Enoch proclaimed, captivating his son and the enchanted Laidey. "In life, she was Brigid Hope, who escaped the cruelty of slavery and dedicated herself to abolishing it, making it her life's mission to free her people from the same fate. She orchestrated a meticulous network of trusted allies to lead her people to freedom."

Sebelius gazed with the same look of admiration as Laidey, and, as Diligence sensed their eyes upon her, she gracefully faded away as if made of sand, the grains dispersing until she was no more. Then, in that same fashion, she reformed before them.

"Welcome, Sebelius Sallow," the spectral beauty greeted him. Bending lower, she looked into the sweetest and most innocent of faces and greeted, "Welcome to you, Adelaide Brindle."

"You know my name?" Laidey replied in surprise.

Diligence chuckled. "In time, you too will come to know all."

Taking in all that had been spoken, Laidey asked pertinently, "Please, Mrs Diligence Sloth, can you help me find my mother?"

The spirit smiled. "I do believe a promise to reunite you with your mother has been made to you," said Diligence, "and in that, you have no reason for my help. You are in very capable hands with these two fine guardians. You are transitioning well," she added, rising to meet Sebelius's gaze.

"Forgive me," Sebelius began awkwardly, "but I fear you credit me too greatly. I cannot accept what has happened — what *is* happening to me. I fear I shall never adjust to it; this is me, unsettled and unhappy for all eternity," Sebelius said mournfully. "I cannot be responsible for the welfare of this child."

"Although sorrow clings to your soul, draw on love and strength to seize control," she assured him, her hand resting on his chest where his heart had once pulsed with the vigour of life. A slew of sensations, akin to a profusion of needles piercing from the inside out, accompanied a weightless drifting.

"Wait! What is happening to me?" Sebelius challenged as he dissolved.

"No, Mr Sallow. Don't leave, I need you," Laidey shouted disapprovingly.

"Don't send him away, please!" his father pleaded, as though it was she that was the cause of this effect.

"This is not my doing. I do believe you are being summoned, Sebelius," Diligence mused as he began to fade away until he was no more.

VIII

Navigating a dimly lit corridor, Sebelius knew nothing of where he was, or how far away, only that he had ventured from his initial point in both space and time, and it could only be guessed if he remained in London at all. Approaching a door on the left, feebly outlined by the dim light beyond, he positioned himself to listen to the muted activity within, punctuated by the subtle indications of life. He placed his hand on the door, the prickle of insubstantiality tingled, reaffirming his detachment from the physical world. Closing his eyes, Sebelius effortlessly walked through the door into the room it guarded.

A cowardly glow streamed out upon the room from the handful of candles that stood to attention in their brass candlesticks, and, in the centre of the luminescence lay a man on a bed fit for the inevitable, his white hair wet with fever and swept back to reveal a lofty head. Whiskers framed the sides of his face, and his features displayed a perpetual agitation — a blend of immense fear, scowling and snarling as if under threat, and vigilant eyes darting in all directions, as though in readiness for potential attacks. His contorted face did not find a moment of repose.

"Away with you! Away with you all!" he repeated, his voice fragile and high-pitched. The *all* to which he referred comprised the room full of men, spirits of men to be more exact, standing around him, inadvertently concealing Sebelius Sallow.

These were men of respectability, of business and commerce, who feasted on their anger as a glutton might gorge ceaselessly at a Christmas buffet. Yet, in their case, the subject was not an illicit pork pie but the man lying in that bed. These men truly were spectres at the feast, for they were all dead and gravely scorned by this man's innumerable misdeeds.

In his chamber they congregated, almost identical to one another, all seamlessly clad in their sombre attire of heavy black, each donning a top hat, deficient of courtesy and displaying utter disregard for the dying man.

As a spirit transitions into the afterlife, they inevitably become privy to the intricate workings of the world, life, and its complexities. It's as though their higher senses unfurl, and every detail on everyone and everything is perfectly labelled, explaining what once was and how it is understood to be.

It was a foreboding house, looking as sad as a diamond tiara on a debutante who adorned rags for a gown. Sebelius understood it had once been a happy home. Large sash windows framed with the most luxurious curtains, now faded and ingrained with dust; exquisitely panelled walls, once vibrant, now paint-peeled, warped, and mangled; richly-mounted portraits succumbed to the damp and cold of England many years ago. The rugs, their fibres once downy in their rich vibrant yellows, reds, blues, and deep purples, now lay threadbare and unbeaten underfoot.

"Away with you! Be gone! Our transactions are concluded gentlemen! You've no business with me!" he raved on. "I will be saved yet!"

The dying man hadn't merely inherited a house, as some might naively assume; instead, he found himself significantly enriched, having gallantly settled a debt to rescue the owner, the industrious Walter Twiselton-Miller, from the clutches of the poorhouse. Though the debt amounted to less than half the value of his home, its inevitable conclusion weighed heavily upon him. What was once a grand and joyous abode, nestled in a faded and stagnant courtyard, seemed now lost amidst the surrounding buildings and warehouses, as if playing a game of hide and seek. The aforementioned Twiselton-Miller, a victim of the tumultuous wave of international trade disruptions and the subsequent decline in exports, succumbed to the very economic challenges that would soon cast his shadow upon the front step of the dying man's office, in search of a financial remedy. It was to be his downfall.

"You came!" the dying man exclaimed with eyes wide that bore into the impenetrable crowd of spectators, which drew Sebelius through them and to the forefront. "You actually came!"

Staring hard into the man's face, barely recognisable, Sebelius saw with immense shock that this was unmistakably the very man who once wore a substantial frock coat and waistcoat with impeccable collar and cuffs. His face was widened by thick white side whiskers, crowned by a well-brushed top hat and a generous mane of fine white hair. The trace of years, nipped by a corset, marked his waist.

"It was you!" Sebelius cried, escalating through various octaves. "You stole the money meant for the poor and needy, leaving me to die in the process."

There came no response, yet the dying man's wrinkled face betrayed a mix of agonising terror and silent protest against the accusations. Sebelius could scarcely believe it; the once formidable presence now seemed feeble and vulnerable, stripped of its former malevolence and replaced by a desperate plea for mercy. Fate had shifted, as this man, who had spent his prime years belittling others to elevate himself, now found himself in dire need of redemption.

"Forgive me, sir, but what is happening here?" Sebelius asked one of the gentlemen among his own kind, who did not fall into the mould of the other gentlemen who looked akin in their dress.

"This man dies tonight. Bear witness to his atrocities. He has harmed all who were unfortunate enough to be darkened by his shadow," the man replied in a deep avenging voice.

From the inflection and tone of both his voice and the beautiful radiance of his skin, he had lived a life as an African American. Never having seen anyone as conspicuous as this creation, Sebelius found himself consistently looking at him, swiftly appraising the opulent attire, his gaze travelling from head to toe. A resplendent green brocade jacket, snugly fitted and adorned with meticulous metallic trim, captured his attention. The breeches, terminating just above the knee, seamlessly transitioned into immaculate white silk stockings, embracing princely legs. The ensemble reached its pinnacle with regal footwear, featuring large embellished bows that adorned the exquisite shoes. However, this subject of much fascination did not once cast his attention in Sebelius's direction. His focus remained fixed on the bed, or rather, the insufferable person who occupied it.

"What is the day?" Sebelius asked him cautiously.

"Christmas Eve," his companion muttered.

"And the year?"

"Eighteen hundred and thirty-six. Fear not, you have not travelled far, Sebelius Sallow, you have been summoned here."

"I have neither travelled to the past nor future," Sebelius uttered to himself. Then, turning to the motionless spectator beside him again, he asked, "So why me... and why this place?"

"Because *he* needs to see you."

"Me? But, why? I am nothing to this man, and I've no bearing on how he chose to live his life," the horologist protested.

"He looks to you to save him," the spirit said without shifting his gaze from the disquieted figure in the bed.

"How?" Sebelius blared incredulously.

"You see the shadows that line the walls of this very room?" the spirit asked. Following the outline of the walls, Sebelius saw the shapes of hooded men, like monks, standing guard, shoulder to shoulder.

"I do."

"They stand in wait. They have waited since this flaxen-haired youth strayed from the path of compassion and upon the desolation of his own kind. They wait for his final breath, and then they will claim his soul, for he shall never know rest."

"How does this involve me?" Sebelius asked inquisitively.

"You were the last to be wronged by him, and he has summoned you here in his thoughts because he perceives you as weak," the spirit continued, elaborating on what the condemned man perceived to be one of the horologist's numerous shortcomings. "He sees in you a forgiving nature, which he deems as weakness, believing you may be swayed by compassion. If there exists one virtuous spirit, who can testify that a soul is worthy of redemption, then it shall be implored, or at the very least, considered. But nothing can save him now. He is truly one of the most contemptible beings, causing harm to all who cross his path. If you were to venture into the passageway now, you would find it teeming with condemning souls, overflowing into every corner of this house; they could fill it thrice over," his companion explained, with an unwavering stare that observed every wince and grimace of discomfort.

"How has this gentleman wronged you?" Sebelius inquired, observing the glimmer of delight reflected in the gaze of his confidante.

"Oh! He hasn't," he responded nonchalantly.

"Therefore your interest in him is…?"

"I have none. My concern is you, Sebelius Sallow," he said with an air of calculated cunning, his eyes still gleaming like the gild of newly minted sovereigns.

"What possible concern could you harbour for me?"

"I come to facilitate your easement," he responded, a warm smile ingratiating his face as he anticipated resounding applause and congratulations for his arrival — a reflex from his earthly calling.

"I require no comfort," Sebelius asserted.

"To offer guidance then," the spirit proposed.

"I seek none. I shall proceed as I always have and resolve this matter within my own mind, crafting my unique pattern of routine, and adapting myself to this place," Sebelius declared. "Who are you?"

"Come now, Sebelius Sallow, remissness is another grave sin. You possess all knowledge of the world around you, invisible to mortal beings, yet you choose to persist in acting like one of them. Who am I?"

In a bid to refine his newly acquired abilities, yet to be applied in this foreign world, Sebelius concentrated and summoned the knowledge to himself. "You are Envy, or in life, you were Ignatius... Ignatius Allerdale. How do I know this?"

"Pray, continue."

"Oh! You were an actor," Sebelius said with surprise, which was immediately to become embellished with greater detail.

"My dear, sir. I was the most esteemed African American actor that there has ever been. You see, I was not the embodiment of envy, but the subject of it," the spirit confessed, "and my life ended as a result of it." He took Sebelius by the hand, and instantly he gleaned all he needed to know about the man who perished by the hands of resentment.

Through this soliloquy, Sebelius learned the tale of Ignatius Allerdale, deposited in his cradle in the heart of New York City in the ninety-ninth year of the previous century. Before the new century had marked its thirtieth year, this charismatic figure, endowed with tremendous wit and impeccable form, boasting exquisite bone structure and a flawless complexion, was tenderly laid to rest in the hallowed grounds of Highgate Cemetery. His rise to stardom as an actor in the United States propelled him to unparalleled success in his adopted home of London. However, it was in this very city that his premature demise unfolded tragically. The treacherous companions with whom he shared the stage twice daily, wielded the very swords that, following a triumphant run of *Othello*, were turned against him. His performance, acclaimed with rave reviews, was said to be delivered with unmatched brilliance.

"I am sorry," Sebelius said mournfully. "You were murdered, and those responsible were never brought to justice."

"Not as sorry as I, but fear not, all that are wronged will wait patiently. The time for retribution shall inevitably come, as it does for this man."

"Pay him no mind, Sebelius," uttered the voice of a gentleman who materialised beside him, bearing a comparable age and style of dress akin to Envy. His chiselled face, powdered as much as the white colossal wigged curls crowning his head, exuded playful authority. "It's truly baffling why he, out of all the spirits in Heaven, was chosen to aid souls navigating the pain and grief of the second stage of their transition. I'm utterly perplexed. Is it even possible to be utterly perplexed? Well, if it is, then count me in. Utterly."

"It is he that should be ignored," Envy declared.

"Who might he be?" Sebelius asked discreetly.

"No one of any real significance, just my spiritual pairing—"

"Come now, we are soul-mates, for our sins," the new attendee announced with eye-rolling dramatics. "How do you do? I am Gratitude. He's just cantankerous because he wasted his life treading the boards, reading other people's words and pretending to be anyone other than himself."

"Says he who spent his existence holding John Adams and Thomas Jefferson's inkwells," Envy sneered jocularly.

"You forgot Washington. I served all three," Gratitude said smugly.

"George Washington always said you were a bad omen!" Envy goaded.

"That is an outrageous fib!" Gratitude protested.

"Well, how do you explain both Adams and Jefferson expiring on the same day *and* on the fourth day of July?"

"I had nothing to do with that!" Gratitude exploded. "James

Monroe, however, well, he never really liked me and I thought that the fourth of July would mark a fitting end, the small matter of him being on the lavatory at the time was merely a coincidence," he smirked coyly.

"You are both here in your capacity as the second stage of grief then?" Sebelius asked, seizing a momentary pause amidst the onslaught of insults.

"Pain and guilt," Envy announced.

"You may save your endeavours, gentlemen. I believe this man is in a greater need of your benevolence than I," Sebelius observed.

The writhing man cried out once more in an attempt of driving away those who awaited. Those familiar with this ruthless moneylender of Finch Lane would struggle to recognise him now. His face, feverish and obscured, still featured thorny brows knitted into a scowling frown, eyes ablaze with fiery intensity. His bearing contorted, body anguished in various convulsions, lips compressed, and veins protruding like ropes on his spindle-shanked neck and temples. His nostrils flared and he sneered like a hunted creature anticipating an imminent assault, his mind so diluted that no one could understand his incoherences.

The candles waned, this tormented man's ears distinguished the murmurs from the thousands of spirits that congregated outside the room. Each spirit spoke in turn, there was a specific order, the breath of death could now be felt upon his face. Each speaker spoke roughly ten incoherent syllables in their turn and then fell silent to the next, crafting a disorienting symphony of unintelligible voices.

"What is going on here?" Sebelius demanded, but no answer came.

The last of the words were exhausted from the corridor and then began within the chamber from the horde of men who gathered around.

"One hundred and forty-eight guineas," said one.

"Four thousand, nine hundred and eighteen pounds," another said.

Again and again, the sums fell from their mouths, then silence rendered them still, so that eventually, all expectancy and attention fell on Sebelius Sallow, especially the man who lay in the bed, with eyes wide, pleading to be spared by the last man whom he had wronged greatly.

"You know what you must do, Sebelius," Envy pointed out.

"But to do so will be to condemn him, will it not?"

"To remain silent will be in violation of justice," Gratitude reinforced, causing the horologist to retreat inside himself.

"Very well," Sebelius said, his heart weighted to the floor. "Eight pounds, fourteen shillings, and seven pence." He looked hard into the face of the man whose expression spoke of immense fear. "I hope for the sake of Christmas, and for that of your soul, that you will be spared." After all, he did not mention the sovereign, a token of sentiment more precious to him than the combined value of all the monetary sums uttered by each apparition.

From where they lined the walls, casting shadows across every nook of the room, the monk-like umbras advanced towards the bed. With a resounding almighty scream, the dying man exhaled his final breath.

His lifeless vessel lay at peace, his soul departed and free, but it wasn't to last. The clink and clang of irons, the metallic thrash of metal, marked the passing of his sentence.

"No! I shall not have it," the newly departed soul wailed frantically. He circled the chamber, in low flight, begging mercy and justice for his soul. "Please, help me!" he warbled, clutching at the fabrics of Sebelius Sallow's coat. A pull of his chains jolted him back, but, defying his fate, he persisted and clung to the cloth of Envy's skirts.

"My lessons fall deafly on the ears of someone such as you, sir," Envy goaded. "Go and cry to Sloth and see how far that takes you."

The clanking grew increasingly deafening, the air thick with the searing heat of the ironmonger's pit. It carried the scent of oily sweat and molten metal, the laborious creation of chains, each link forged by every individual sin and minuscule unkindness, ready now to bear its burden for eternity.

"Enslaved, restrained, and encased in twin irons," Envy stipulated.

His soul wailed and sobbed, departing life just as his infant-self had entered it.

"The more people have, the more they feel hard done by," concluded Gratitude.

"What now?" Sebelius voiced loudly over the thrash of the man's cries and clashing metals. He could barely look, the brutality was akin to a pack of wolves set against a chained bear.

"He must yield," Gratitude declared as Sebelius saw an unmistakable upsurge of excitement upon his face. "He is broken, but not yet cowed."

"This is not my fate, it cannot be for me!" protested the tormented soul as the shackles of his wrongdoings writhed and whipped without restraint. His trespasses were beyond his recognition, his conscience was clear.

Past Three O'Clock

With an almighty crack of the chain, like a whip reigning an unruly beast, the man yielded, took to his knee, and the hordes of spectators laughed and goaded him, comforted by the knowledge that he would never rest long enough to ever know peace again.

IX

The chamber of torment dissolved around them and Sebelius was summoned back to a familiar place — a place that exuded life, even when empty. How could a space filled with innumerable timepieces, all ticking to the rhythm of the same second, not feel eternally alive? His little shop was outlined by dim light, borrowed from the illuminations spilling from Ludlow Hill beyond the window pane. Yet all was very still; the faithful hands of each clock froze just a little past three o'clock, ceasing the moment that Sebelius Sallow was called from their reach, except for one. 'London Waits' played its merry tune that marked the eleventh hour.

"Mr Sallow! You have returned," Adelaide Brindle exploded with excitement at the sight of him. "I called and called for you, but you never came. I thought you were always to go wherever you were wanted or needed."

"My apologies, little Laidey," he said pensively, "but I was needed elsewhere. Trust me when I say I would rather have been here with you and Father." He ran his forearm over his troubled brow.

"Have you found Mother?" she asked with a face glowing with expectancy.

"Not yet, but we will," he replied, watching as heartfelt disappointment caused the child's eyes to gaze to the floor. "I am doing all I can to find her." He knelt down to meet her. "I appear to have a lot to learn, and there is a higher purpose guiding me. If you believe in me, I will reunite you with your mother."

Adelaide looked into his honest face and said, "With all my heart, I believe in you, Mr Sallow." He knew that she meant it, what radiated from her hand told him so.

"Where is Father?" he asked, rising back to his customary perpendicular stance.

"I am here, my boy," said a voice from within the workshop. "I failed to tell you that the order and method you've brought is wonderful."

"I had a lot of time on my hands when you were away," Sebelius said, coming to a sudden halt as there was a fierce rattle of the front door handle, causing Adelaide to gasp and Enoch to look perplexingly in the direction of his son.

"Burglars!" Enoch exclaimed with vehemence.

"On Christmas Eve?"

"What better time, when all in London are tucked up at home in the embrace of their families," he reasoned.

"There appears to be only one of them!" Then, moving towards the door, Sebelius shouted, "We are here, please leave or we shall call for a constable."

"Sebelius, he cannot hear you, or see you for that matter," his father explained.

"Could we perhaps give him a little fright?" Sebelius asked, playfully fluttering the fingers of his right hand before his lips. "How do we make ourselves seen?"

"You have to want to be seen," Enoch said earnestly.

"Wonderful!" came the buoyant response.

"They have to want to see you in return," his father interjected.

"Oh! Well, no one really wishes to see a ghost," Sebelius concluded disappointedly. After pondering a short while he asked, "Have you ever been seen?"

"I've never been seen by a living soul. I sat with you many a day, through spring, summer, autumn, until this very morning. I wanted you to see me, but feared you might be frightened. Similarly, I believe that you wanted to see me, but I sensed that you might fear encountering me."

"I suppose that is true. I longed to see you but I would have been afraid, although you did nothing but love and care for me in life and so would do no harm to me in death," Sebelius reasoned.

The unyielding rattle ricocheted through the shop, as it quivered in response to the tenacious assaults on the door handle. Whoever sought entry was unwavering in their persistence, and, as faithful as ever, Adelaide placed herself before Sebelius, as his protector.

Gripping his son by the elbow, Enoch attempted to stop him from moving towards the door. "He will not see you. Only when both the spirit and mortal beings desire to see and be seen can the spirit manifest itself in the tangible world."

The muggy yellow light, born of the frail orb-like gleam emanating from the lamps, dimmed with obscurity as the assailant positioned himself at the window. Peering through the pane, his face cradled in cupped hands, he cast a foreboding silhouette against the dim-lit backdrop.

"Sebelius! No—" his father called with urgency as his son

approached the window hastily, fixing his gaze into the hands that concealed the face of the man on the opposite side of the glass.

"Sebelius?" whispered the glad voice through a smile of relief, belonging to someone whose eyes rested on the face they longed to see. However, the joy turned to sudden fright as he pulled back, realising that the face, though familiar and affectionately known, was no longer part of this world. He staggered backward, his eyes frozen wide with the welling up of emotions. His throat betrayed an obvious gulp, and, as he gasped, the air escaped his lips like the smoke of a discharged gun. Doubt momentarily paralysed him, but, summoning the strength to breathe again, he did, and the sensation pained him.

"Aubrey!" Sebelius shrieked. The face Sebelius yearned to see was now drained of its usual exuberance. "I am a monster, a thing of nightmares, he can no longer bear to look at me."

"Take me away from this place!" Bravington's urgent plea shattered through the bitter night air, reaching the ears of the hansom driver who, muffled against the cold, revealed only his watchful eyes. With a swift nod, the driver whipped up his horse and they were away at an indignant canter through the snowy street, leaving Sebelius to shoot through the shop front and take to his heels in a desperate chase.

The two-wheeler, harnessed with its stealthy and well-conformed steed at the helm, manoeuvred beautifully. It was all Sebelius could do to keep up and he fell short, his gusto weakened by his inadequacy, so he could only watch the carriage continue down Fleet Street.

Shame from his encounter settled in, shock, denial, pain, and guilt transformed into bargaining. Inwardly, he pleaded for a second chance, vowing to cherish every precious moment life bestowed upon him. Though the hansom lingered in the distance, its trajectory leading toward the Strand, Sebelius contemplated resuming his pursuit before ultimately deciding against it.

"Is that all you have to give?" erupted the sneering voice of a slender figure materialising to his left. His bulbous head, lacking natural covering, wore a coarse wig crafted intricately from the tail of his beloved steed — an equine companion elevated to the esteemed rank of consul during his Roman reign. "Well, is it?" The Emperor, draped in the typical toga attire, presented sunken eyes ablaze with arrogance.

"So, you are—" Sebelius asked nonchalantly.

"Wrath, naturally," he began in a snide, drawn-out fashion. "I was, in my time, a rotter, it is true, but I am now reformed, angry no more, so I can assist you in your transition, you might say." He spoke in a highly strung, twitchy fashion, punctuating his words with little sneering laughs, yet somehow, Sebelius was more fearful of this apparition than any other he had encountered or observed.

"Can you help me back to my former life? My life may not have been much, but it was mine and I would give anything for Aubrey Bravington to speak to me, to notice and regard me as he once did," Sebelius pleaded.

"No, not possible, there is no going back," the Emperor tittered callously, sliding a reptilian finger under his mane to ease the discomfort with a steady scratch. "Come now! This Aubrey Bravington has seen you once already, so what are you waiting for?" he said, smiling with a creepy intention of kindness, which was his most atrocious characteristic. It was a scheming, evil grin, akin to a cat revelling in the killing of a beautiful red-breasted robin, that is, if a cat possessed all the expressive facial nuances of a human.

"Imperator Gaius, may I borrow your horse?" Sebelius requested humbly.

"I think not." He giggled with a pleasing glint in his eyes.

"I thank you, regardless," Sebelius replied excitedly as he mounted the saddle. With a cry, he commanded the animal to pursue the carriage.

Sebelius charged in the direction of the hansom that carried Bravington, who was so dismayed he sat in a bath of his own perspiration. His mind at war, he battled with the reliability of his senses.

"No, it couldn't be him. If not him, then who?" Bravington garbled in various repeated fashions as he grappled with thoughts of the face he saw in the window — a face resembling Sebelius Sallow's yet not quite. Simultaneously, he tried desperately to push the encounter from his mind but he couldn't.

With eyes tightly shut, Bravington desperately compared the Sebelius he knew in life to the ghostly apparition before him. His friend had such captivating features, not of rugged masculinity but of classical precision, with ivory skin and delicately sculpted contours. His eyes, large and limpid, with flawless whites and a hazel glint in their depths, were the very windows to his soul. Despite his immense heart and his struggle to express outward emotion, it was through his eyes that Sebelius conveyed his inner strength, beauty, and kindness. Though his face and mouth often concealed his feelings behind internal barriers, his eyes shimmered with emotion. When he smiled, it was as if a radiant sun had emerged, capable of melting snow-capped mountains. These moments held a magical allure for Bravington, and, though the vision of Sebelius before him was altered, it remained unmistakably his dear friend.

With thrill, and sheer terror, Sebelius thrashed the saddle down the Strand, careening into Whitehall. In a desperate bid to capture Bravington's attention, Sebelius rode alongside the carriage, bellowing out to his friend. Despite the intensity of his shouts, he remained unseen. He raced the carriage past Westminster, where the fragile remnants of Parliament stood charred, supported by scaffold and hopeful promises of resurrection after the devastating fire of two years before. Down Parliament Street, glimpses of the Thames fluttered, its frigid waters outlined by the flickering lamps of the Samaritans' cordon, guarding against further revellers perishing on the ice. The cab thrashed along Millbank and thrust right, into Horseferry Road, they soon found themselves navigating a warren of streets until the carriage finally halted outside an enchanting square of houses, erected in the previous century and encircled by a gracefully winding road.

This square boasted a circular row of refined, evenly-bricked houses, each adorned with black railings; modest when compared to the striking brilliance of the church dedicated to Queen Anne, proudly standing at the square's centre.

The square witnessed a gathering of bodies, preparing for midnight Mass, with the choir's carols resonating as their voices gently echoed against the house bricks and the melody danced around the curvature of the road.

"Here, take this," Bravington shouted at the cab driver, tossing his fare into the expectant hand. Without a word of thanks or any accustomed greetings of the season, the artist hurled himself towards his front door. The hansom pulled away, and, almost as if temptation lured him, the erstwhile passenger glanced back, spotting Sebelius Sallow standing on the pavement's edge.

"Aubrey!" Sebelius called out with his hand outstretched.

"Sebelius?" Bravington pleaded in return, but terror overwhelmed any concern for his friend or the figure resembling him. He slammed the door, fastened every bolt, and slid down to the floor in shameful fear.

"The next time I refuse you the use of my horse, you will respect my command," Wrath remonstrated Sebelius, standing next to his steed, while the horologist, too devastated to care, looked on.

"I thought myself rid of you!" Sebelius retorted bitterly.

"It's a good thing that Temperance is faithful—" Wrath pontificated.

"Temperance? You mean to say that you have been paired with your horse in the afterlife?" Sebelius said snidely, having no time for niceties.

"And what of it? Temperance was more faithful to me than my wife ever was. Besides, she makes me a much nicer soul. I only hope you find your happily ever after. Then perhaps you might be more contented in your new life."

"He was my soul-mate," Sebelius said sorrowfully, looking at the house that acted as protector to Aubrey Bravington from... well... Sebelius himself.

Wrath bore a look of absolute disgust. "Oh my, and you mock me for my horse!"

"Do you not have any other spirits to aggravate?" Sebelius sighed.

"You've much to learn. If you chase the living as if you were still one yourself, your endeavours will be ineffective," the former ruler said with a caustic, gleeful sneer. "I will gladly teach you. You and

I can venture into that house right now—" Wrath said, waving his robe in his hand in a physical request for Sebelius to take it and continue along with him.

"I shan't go with you. Besides, I couldn't face it. Twice he has seen me, and twice he has had that look of horror on his face," Sebelius explained.

"Oh, come, it would be most enjoyable. You and I could show that living creature that we can scare him so that gooseflesh would break out on gooseflesh." Glee shone upon his antagonist's face. "We can show him real horrors."

"Stay clear of him, you understand? I don't care who you think you are or who you were in your time, but take care because I will not be trifled with, especially when it comes to Aubrey Bravington."

"Very well, I shall say no more about it." In the stomach of Wrath, there stuck out a ghostly dagger, the very same that ended his mortal days. He gripped the handle with both hands and pushed it further into his stomach. "You cut me deep, Sebelius," he said, doubling forward and staggering this way and that before falling to the floor in apparent agony.

"Spirit, I did not mean—" Sebelius said shamefully, but the vitriolic laughter of the most sinister kind erupted, and Wrath emerged from the floor stronger and more fearful in his puny human-looking frame.

"Well done, Sebelius. You are transitioning well! You are beginning to feel, and acquaint yourself with anger. Isn't it marvellous?" he drawled malevolently, his mirth growing louder and louder, causing the snow on the ground to swirl into a frenzy. The mortal citizens, oblivious to the spirits walking among them, hurried through the church doors for shelter from this sudden blizzard.

"I just wanted him to care for me!" Sebelius exploded amidst the snowstorm that raged greater with Wrath's abrasive chortling.

"Why, Sebelius, he does care for you! Didn't you know?" The gruesome creature sniggered and his cackling grew still.

"What is happening to me?" Sebelius bellowed into the blindness of snow and against the deafening guffaw. In the icy swirl of cold and ice, Sebelius began to fall away into tiny particles.

"Merry Christmas, Sebelius, wherever you are," a feminine voice rang out amongst the chaos with all the sentiment of love. It was this voice that was drawing him away.

"You are being summoned, Sebelius! You are being called! You must go!" Wrath exclaimed, his voice taut and booming, overpowering the din of disruption around them.

And with that, Sebelius diminished.

X

The gentleman sat by his hearth, savouring the last puffs of his pipe while contemplating the print in his newspaper. His wife occupied the window seat, gazing outside, and Sebelius stood in a corner, momentarily forgetting his immortal spirit and the shroud of death that concealed him.

"Merry Christmas, Sebelius, wherever you are." The same deep affection resonated in the suffocation of hushed tones. Sebelius looked on as this female beauty hummed a Christmas melody while drawing angels on the window pane with her finger. Her face lacked the regularity of Christmas joy and the warmth of complexion, yet her nature radiated charm and geniality. Her large brown eyes were remarkably bright and caring, and, to look upon her you might never see again a more gracious and delicate creature in your life.

A tut emanated from the fireside chair. "Must you?" The bombastic, urbane gentleman continued to smoke, deriving as much pleasure from watching the blue emissions travel and diffuse across the room as he did from making his wife feel insufficient and ineffectual.

"It is always so much worse at Christmas." She continued her hum, finger crafting angelic friends with wings and halos.

The sound of locking doors confirmed that the servants were preparing to retire for the evening, but then came a knock at the drawing room door.

"Begging your pardon, sir?" the youngest of their maids asked nervously as she hovered in the door. "Cook's closing down the kitchen for the night and we too are preparing for bed, is there anything else you or m'lady might be wanting before we are to bed?"

"No, thank you, Bexley, that will be all," the lady in the window gave pardon.

"Thank you, ma'am." She dipped a slight curtsy.

"Sleep well, won't you," her mistress bade her, "and Merry Christmas."

"Wait a moment," the man in the chair commanded. "You might replenish this?" His request came with an arm outstretched, his meaty hand holding out a pipe.

Obligingly, dipping another bob and taking the offering, the maid knocked out the spent tobacco into the fire and filled his smoking vessel with the golden Perique strands of his naval days. His eyes watched her intently, while his wife's eyes bored into him. As for Bexley, she was to be married in the new year, and she counted the days with all the excitement that belonged by rights to Christmas and birthdays, until she could leave the home of her mistress and her husband, Colonel Cecil-Yule. Their beautiful home was a sullen place.

This ghastly man, to whom his wife tethered all her aspirations and desires of youth, presented an obstinate countenance, both stern of face and heart. Draped now in the simplicity of a dressing gown, his naval uniform, adorned with medals and golden epaulettes of an honoured British officer from the Napoleonic Wars, was preserved in an enormous portrait above the fire by the little-known artist, Aubrey Bravington. The oil was not even dry on the canvas, and the musky, oil-scent of the paint still perfumed the room.

The woman possessed astonishing grace, retaining her imposing and noble appearance even after more than two decades of marriage to the disapproving naval hero.

Bexley took her leave, and the officer's wife continued to speak out loud, perpetually speaking to herself, as was so often the case. He sat in his own silence, engrossed in the fresh aroma of printed ink, while she gazed wistfully out the window, her forehead rested upon the glass. "Do you not think, Joshua?"

"Effie, Effie, Effie. Every year, on Christmas Eve, your mind wanders and this mood sets in." His patronising resonance was underlined with a roll of the eyes.

"Christmas is a difficult time for many, trimming all that is bare with decorations and dispelling all the darkness of the year with light. Yet with all that glimmer and sparkle, it's a time of stark exposure, where emotions intensify. For the less fortunate, poverty feels more profound. The hungry, hungrier. The friendless, lonelier." She grieved for herself over the latter of her three observations.

"You should thank God that you do not know the chilling grasp of poverty, the searing burn of hunger, or the overwhelming flood of abandonment. You were delivered of a husband to take care of these concerns!" The jibe came from a bowed mouth framed by a well-trimmed moustache and an exquisite square jaw.

"I already had one of those when I married you. I just miss him so. Is that a crime?"

"No," he began supportively, carefully examining the aftermath of the financial instability in the newly formed Texan republic post-revolution and its independence from Mexico. "Perhaps you should have fought more passionately for him, then you would have no need to miss him."

"I chose you! I abandoned Sebelius for you! It means nothing to you, does it? I mean nothing to you!"

"Euphemia, my dear—"

"Euphemia?" Sebelius gasped with a stabbing pain where his heart used to beat and a thwack to his gut, which had likewise lost its function. "It cannot be?"

"Do not 'my dear' me," she snapped, dwelling on where the man she once loved had vanished. Colonel Joshua Cecil-Yule was as debonair and genial a seaman as you could ever wish to meet. As time passed, his capacity for considerable fury and grudge-bearing became more apparent. This darker side, however, seemed exclusively aimed at his wife, unnoticed by others but certainly felt by Euphemia. A subtle moroseness overcame him, as if an invisible hand had stolen the smile from any occasion that would bring joy to any other person. Amid these sulking spells, he dwelled in the deepest murk for days on end. The man she knew from her youth shone brighter than his naval buttons, but upon his return, post-combat and with no real purpose following injury, his inclination towards darkness, solitude, and secrecy became his natural bearing.

"Father!" Sebelius exploded aloud and called for him twice more. "Enoch Sallow, I am summoning you!" he commanded tersely but opted to change tack. "Might I kindly ask that divine intervention that has had me popping up all over London," —

bringing along the most perplexing spirits with it, he thought — "please summon my father here, immediately?"

"I am here, Sebelius," his father replied ruefully, materialising beside his son.

"You told me she had died!"

"Sebelius, I can explain."

"All that you told me was a lie!" Sebelius condemned his father, who hung his head in shame. "It was my earliest memory, my very first. You took me aside, sat me down, and said, 'My boy, my dear Sebelius, I need you to be a big, brave boy.' When I asked why, you looked so sad, you convincingly said, 'Your Mama is gone, she is now with the angels.'"

"I did it to protect you!"

"You truly believed that telling a four-year-old child that his mother had died was the best form of protection?"

Frustration consumed Enoch, conveyed as he gripped his son's arm. "As you are so sure of everything, would you like me to show you what I have been protecting you from? Would you like me to show you? Very well!" Enoch blasted and all around them blared intensely white as they were transported back to a distant past.

"There she is!" Enoch pointed to the female who was unmistakably the younger version of the woman who occupied the window. "Euphemia Bonham, the sole daughter of the celebrated Major Jasper Bonham. Your grandfather heroically perished in battle, leaving her heartbroken—"

"I understand how that feels," came Sebelius's scornful retort.

"Sebelius, please."

"I feel an intensity of such emotion, far greater than when I walked that side of the divide, it is killing me all over again. The more I learn, the greater the rage, and I do not care for it," Sebelius explained bitterly.

"The loss of her father was immeasurable, but she was well provided for — a young woman of means. It was before your grandfather's death that she was introduced to Joshua Cecil-Yule, at some military event or other. They fell passionately in love and she was promised to him. Her captain was sent to fight in the Napoleonic Wars and was presumed dead, leaving her heartbroken for a second time. As an apprentice horologist to my father, I met her at her family's home and, in a matter of weeks, she took my name but never, as I later discovered, gifted me her heart."

Time elapsed around them and Sebelius witnessed the moments after his birth, where it was evident that he bonded them with a mutual love.

"I'm leaving, Enoch," Effie announced as the scene melted away into the final juncture where he should ever see his wife again.

"Leaving? Why?" Enoch pleaded, aggrieved.

It soon became clear that Effie Bonham, the love of Enoch Sallow's life, had only ever borrowed his name, shamefully returning it battered, bruised, and unfit for any purpose, much like his heart. And the reason? Well, that was because her gallant love had miraculously returned. Amidst the boom of cannon strikes, the thunderous fog of musket smoke, and the persistent drum of a forward march, Captain Cecil-Yule guided his men bravely. Thought to be lost, along with his memory, in the chaotic tumult of war, he had returned. She could not thank God strongly or hard enough.

"We have found her, sir," came the oppressive drawl of his valet's voice, delivered with heavy-lidded eyes. "We have telegrammed the young lady, and she, well, in fact, she has just arrived, but I feel it only fair to mention, sir—" but Captain Cecil-Yule would hear no more, for he was away on his heels and running to the door of his study.

"Effie, my love, I have returned to you, and here you are without a hair out of place since I bid you farewell," he said, his earnest eyes wide as he embraced her and thought that he should never let her go. "Now, we can be married, my love."

The gallant soldier spoke, clasping her hands, and didn't stop speaking, leaving her not a moment to respond. He had a lifetime of sentiment to deliver, and nothing, nor no one, could stop him, until that fateful knock at the door.

"Sorry to intrude, sir," the housekeeper interrupted, "but he won't settle, madam. He is in want of his mother." And as the four-year-old Sebelius saw his mother, he was away to her arms.

There was a stern look and a disapproving scowl, followed by the pertinent question on the military leader's part. "What is that?"

"This is Sebelius. This is my son," she said proudly, but, in an instant, her pride turned to shame.

"You're not leaving me, Effie! You're my wife!" Enoch blasted with the intensity of what would define so much of Sebelius's childhood.

Undeterred, she packed hurriedly, matching the urgency pulsating in Enoch's chest. "I *am* leaving you, Enoch," she asserted defiantly.

In the face of impending loss, Enoch struck a final blow. "You won't be taking my son! Sebelius stays with me!" he declared.

She turned, with tears betraying her innermost pain. "I never intended to separate you from your son. He will stay," she conceded, defeated.

Enoch's heart now ached for his son, as not only had she reneged on her marriage vows, but she had done the same with her professed motherly love.

"You had no intention of taking him, did you?" Aghast and torn, Enoch understood her true intentions. "The valiant Captain Cecil-Yule wants you, but not our son, of course." Relief soon followed, for he would have sooner sold his soul to the lowest bidder than to shatter the heart of his son; that was as precious to him as his wife's.

As his wife made her exit, Enoch was clear in his mind. "I will grant you a speedy divorce, get your new man to set the wheels in motion immediately. But, if you walk through that door, Effie, you will cease to exist in Sebelius's life. I won't let him question why he wasn't enough to keep you or believe you chose a greater love than his own. He'll be told that you have died, and that you had nothing but love for him. Never attempt to contact him. It would hurt him more than your leaving now. You may go."

The door closed behind her.

"I'm not proud that those were my parting words, but clarity struck in an instant. Loss's pain was inevitable. I couldn't shield you from that. Yet I could influence how you perceived yourself. In a person's death, you can move on, cherish and lament the past, paint hazy scenes of a future which they might have shared. When abandoned, you linger in the hurt of never feeling quite good enough, forever constructing a future to prove your worth to yourself — and all those around you. Sebelius Sallow, you have always been good enough."

These seamlessly blended memories, in no particular fashion, made one thing clear; before the noble commander was sent to war, he exuded wholesomeness, sincerity, and gallantry. However, the disillusionment of battle, coupled with a critical moment where injuries stifled his breathing and resuscitation failed, transformed him profoundly. Retrieving his first love held some semblance of the world he left behind, but upon discovering her to be married and a mother to a child that might have been his, she lost the enchantment he once attributed to her, becoming a prize to be claimed but not wanted. Effie was now his, retrieved on his terms.

With the dissolution of the grim past surrounding them, Sebelius found himself once again in the present, and in the presence of his mother and the man for whom she had abandoned their once-happy family. They stood only a rabbit's whisker from one another as their rage intensified. They blamed one another for so much.

"You're like all the rest, my dear — walking through life with the belief that everything you possess and hold dear, even the people you love, will never be taken away — until they are. Then, you cry, scream, and lament, only to eventually return to the same lunacy of complacency," her husband asserted.

"You understood. I did it all for you. I left behind my son and a man who loved me boundlessly," Effie lambasted.

"You soon repaired your broken heart," he sniggered.

She retaliated by raising her small hand and striking the side of his arm. "I never took you for being so soulless!"

His reflexes tightened around her wrist, igniting Sebelius's anger into a raging fury. Candles flickered in their holders and the fire in the grate dimmed as his fury cast shifting shadows, animating the room around them. With a forceful motion, her husband flung her to the floor, releasing his grip.

"Sebelius, no!" Enoch yelled. "We cannot involve ourselves in matters of their world!"

Sebelius blustered himself forward, pushing the flat of his hand against Colonel Cecil-Yule's chest, their noses nearly touching and, with wide eyes that blared out with fear, the commander saw the ghostly face of Sebelius Sallow, and let out an almighty scream that was enough to cause the newly retired staff, who were abed, to come running.

"Step away, Sebelius," his father commanded. "You have done enough."

He knew what he had to do. Sebelius waited until he was sure that dread had penetrated the commander's very core, and then he submitted.

"Sebelius, I did it all to protect you, I promise," his father said mercifully.

"How do I get away from this place?" Sebelius demanded.

"Come, my boy, I will take you—"

"No!" he barked, "I need to be alone." His look was enough to discourage any defiance and so Enoch told him.

"Think of a place you would like to visit or a face you would like to see, and there you shall be," Enoch advised.

Shutting his eyes tightly, Sebelius vanished, appearing where he very nearly wanted to go. He stood upon the spot from where he last saw his friend dash fearfully into his house. The snow lay hushing every sound the city ever knew, aside from the gentle singing that emanated from the church that loomed behind him.

It was those harmonious tunes and voices that went a long way in soothing a tensely nervous Bravington. Although he would never call himself a superstitious man, and certainly never allowed the thought of ghosts to tax any part of his mind, he found himself cradled in his fireside chair, nestled in the security of his locked bedchamber.

The candles soothed with their silent glow but provided no solace to a bewildered Bravington, and neither did the fire that danced merrily on logs thickly shrouded in bark. Their flicker surged with an intensity that made the candles weep and shadows rise in recognition of Sebelius's presence.

He sat up with a start. "I feel you, whoever you are, and know you are here," he said with false courage, and false it surely was as he had not the resolve to turn and face the room. "I feel you and ask kindly that you leave. I bid you no ill will, and I trust you bear none to me, so I ask you again, please leave me alone."

The fabrics in the room stirred with intention as the weighty sense of Sebelius's ethereal presence dissipated. Bravington let out a sigh of relief before succumbing to quiet sobs.

XI

The initial hint of winter's dawn was lazily emerging, and Christmas morning greeted the dimly lit figures of early tradesmen and charladies scurrying to assume their positions. Their movements were bleary and subdued under the prismatic London mist. They shuffled in silence, except for the occasional exchanges of "Merry Christmas" and the rustling of heavy clothing, a welcomed barrier against the day's bitter cold. Those well-wrapped, merely tipped their hats, moved by the reluctance to expose their throats to the frigid air and its deadly venom.

"Cor blimey, Mrs Bung, it's cold enough for drawers this morning, in no mistake," the landlady shouted from the doorway of her public house.

"Drawers, y'say, Mrs Perkins? I've got meself three pairs on, and one of those is the ol' man's," the char cackled in reply to her employer.

"Oh, you are a card. I swear this bitter air has teef this very day," she crowed over the rattle of a mop in the bucket she was holding.

"Well, I wish they'd lend them to the ol' man, he has a blessed awful time with chewin' his meat." She chortled, and they both cackled. "Leave that! You'll be doin' me out of a job, Mrs Perkins."

"And where the bloomin' 'eck do you fink you've been?" the landlady bawled, staring right at Sebelius who stood in the courtyard before The Lamb and Flag public house.

In an attempt to reply, Sebelius stumbled over his words when suddenly the downtrodden figure of her husband, the subject of the landlady's scorn, emerged straight through him from behind.

"This is a fine time, I must say, to be turning back up here after the graft has been done," she scolded, then turned to her companion. "As if I haven't got enough to do! He leaves during the Christmas Eve rush, leaving me to deal with that sham of a pantomime that *he* played a song and dance for us to hold," Mrs Perkins berated.

"You're in for it now, Stanley Perkins, I don't need to be a clairvoyant to know that!" Mrs Bung smirked. "And wha' in 'eavens are you wearin'?" She cackled so hard it caused her ribs to hurt, not that they could be detected under the many layers of clothing and years of relentless indulgence.

"Don't you start, Maud, I get enough grief off her," Stanley Perkins retaliated, holding the door so that the domestic could get straight to her duties. He looked back. "Aren't you coming in?" he said looking straight at Sebelius.

The lonely spirit looked around him.

The man looked expectantly. "Yes, you. You are very welcome here," Stanley said with a chuckle.

Sebelius couldn't help but be impressed by a mere glance at this man. He had a square, massive face covered with even stubble and thoughtful eyes under heavy brows, along with the classic definition of an obstinate jawline. Stanley Perkins exuded sincerity of character, a hardworking man with a mind rooted in strong principles. Stern at first glance but straightforward, inwardly quiet, and formidable. Such were the impressions he left, especially considering his unusual outfit — he wore a dress.

Nothing uncommon at this festive time, for he was the pantomime dame, and this year, in honour of Queen Victoria, whose royal derrière had only graced the British seat for a mere six months, he was the grand embodiment of regality bordering on the fantastical, dressed as Queen Elizabeth, that great Tudor queen. She was presented exactly how she wouldn't have been, but the effort was commendable. Two large stuffed pillowcases formed his impressive chest, concealed beneath a sumptuous patchwork gown of rich, multicoloured tones. The gown cascaded in voluminous layers that trailed gracefully behind, an exaggerated lace ruff around the neck adding to the opulence befitting a sovereign lady.

Each square or remnant of fabric had been donated by locals in the destruction of old garments and given new life; local dressmakers contributed willingly, using the valuable waste that sat on the cutting room floor. Crafted by Mrs Perkins, the gown bore intricate embroidery to make the patches flow as one. It shimmered with every sway and motion. Sebelius stared intently at the small crown fastened atop a towering flame-red wig. Under the powdered face and enormous painted lips, he saw a man that was kind of heart. How many men would do this every year to bring joy to his patrons and much needed funds to the poor and destitute?

Mr Perkins held the door open in a welcoming gesture as he listened to both ladies lambast him for letting out the fire's comforting warmth. Yet, as he looked at the horologist, a gratified expression adorned his strong features.

"Now, you just settle yourself down there," he said after excusing himself into a small, cosy parlour which served as the private quarters he shared with his wife. There was a small fire, and he warmed himself while preparing a strong pot of tea.

Introductions were made, first by the mortal man of much wit and charisma. "I'm Stanley Perkins, or Patty Cake as I'm commonly known, especially around this time of year. Not only am I the publican of this fine establishment, but the baker next door." Seeing the look on the spirit's bearing he roared, "Don't tell me you've not heard of Yeast and West Bakers? Well, I am dumbfounded." Patty Cake broke into a laugh.

The lonely apparition made his acquaintance and gave a blow-by-blow account from the moments that led up to reuniting with Aubrey Bravington to the moment he stood before the doors of the public house.

"How is it that you can see me when others cannot?" Sebelius asked.

"I see you, Sebelius Sallow, because I possess a... sort of gift, passed down from my mother, and it's not something I understand myself, nor discuss openly," he said without embarrassment. "Don't mistake me, I have no shame surrounding my talents. But how does a person explain that they converse with the departed?"

The inquisitive Mrs Perkins placed the flat palm of her hand against the door, followed by an ear, listening intently to the deep tone of her husband's voice. She knocked on the door and poked her head through: "Is everything well, Pat?" she asked quietly.

"Aye, it is," he said with a reassuring look.

"Another visitor?"

"Indeed. Sebelius Sallow, this is my wife, Mrs Perkins. Bessie, to her nearest and dearest. Bessie, this is Sebelius Sallow."

"I'm very pleased to meet you, Mr Sallow," she said, looking awkwardly at the empty chair.

"The pleasure is mine," Sebelius responded. "Can she see or hear me?" Sebelius asked the baker.

He shook his head. "Mr Sallow is very pleased to make your acquaintance, Bessie."

"I will leave you gentlemen to it," she said, giving a little bow of her head in the direction of the empty chair. She always supported her husband's gift yet failed to understand it. In many ways, she shut her mind off to death and preferred to fixate on living. For her, knowing little about a contentious subject led to a more contented outcome.

"It appears to me that you're in a bit of a quandary," the baker mused. "You are caught between two worlds, Sebelius. Firstly, there's the fondness you have for this Aubrey Bravington, and secondly, you have discovered your mother alive and well, and living with this blaggard, who I have a mind to put my belt to."

"Please, Mr Perkins, we must have none of that! Besides, he is a soldier and a horrid creature," Sebelius interjected.

Stanley Perkins erupted in a loud and hearty chuckle. "You needn't worry about me, Sebelius Sallow," he said with great mirth. "I may spend a good deal of Christmas in women's skirts, but the other eleven months of the year are devoted to hosting bare-knuckle prize fighting in this very establishment, and I haven't been bested yet. And, like I said, my friends call me Patty Cake."

"I am glad to consider you a friend, Mr Cake, or is it Mrs Cake, I'm confused," Sebelius stumbled awkwardly.

The baker laughed. "Patty is just fine."

"I don't really have a soul to rely on at the moment, Patty" he concluded, glumly.

"You can rely on this soul." Patty paused and thought for a while. "Who inherits, now that you are no more?"

"I don't actually know." Sebelius took a moment to contemplate. "I had never given it a thought. I never really prepared for my... death." He sank a little. "Why do you ask?"

"Your assets could be the saving grace that could rescue your mother from her current predicament," he said assuredly.

Round and round the room, Sebelius drifted and swirled, filling the air with mournful exclamations. It was a pitiful and frightful sight for Patty to witness such a pure spirit so uproarious with pain. He insisted the spirit be calm, but the agitation of uncertainty about his worldly possessions — so very few, but still of considerable value — weighed heavily on him. Bricks and mortar, a commodity that always seemed secure, now felt uncertain in death, for dying intestate meant that any possessions would be disposed of, with any monies swallowed up by a government that always seemed to prosper more greatly than the public it served.

Patty pondered the situation logically. After listening intently to Sebelius's anxieties, the only answer was to head to Westminster, namely to the home of Aubrey Bravington. Having someone of Bravington's stature on their side might help sort out the affairs of Sebelius's property, rescue his mother, ensure a proper farewell at his funeral, and potentially uncover information about Adelaide Brindle's mother too.

"You're going out?" Mrs Perkins, who held a silver tray with two glasses filled with port, shrieked as her husband hurried through the door of their parlour. "But I brought these for you and Mr Sallow!"

"No time, my dear," he replied, leaning down to grace his wife's forehead with a kiss. He swivelled sharply on his heel, grabbed the glass, and effortlessly gulped down its contents.

"What about Mr Sallow?" she asked as he pivoted once more, snatching the second glass and executed the same swift gulp. "He says 'thank you'." He smirked, leaving her with a smear of his lipstick just above her brows.

Thrusting his robust, not-so-regal frame into the road, he summoned a hansom to slow to a careful stop.

"My, my, my, if it isn't Queen Patty of the West End. What brings you out so early on this cold Christmas morning? Is Mallam's having a sale on frilly bloomers?" the runtish driver asked, sneering.

"Never you mind! You get me to Smith's Square on the double, Sidney Betsy, and it's Mr Perkins to you. Remember that," Patty Cake barked, and Sidney gulped as his passenger ascended into the cab without delay.

"He is no great friend of yours?" Sebelius inquired as the carriage began to stir toward Westminster.

"Not ruddy likely," Patty seethed.

"You make it quite obvious in your manner." Sebelius smiled.

"I know him of old. Harmless on the grander scale, but they are the ones you need to watch. They're the kind that come at you from behind. When a man such as he, who is lower than a worm's privates, wishes to take the rise out of me — when, in truth, he only feels big when he makes others feel small, especially women — then I have cause to make my feelings known."

There was a comfortable silence and Patty Cake observed the small, thin frame of Sebelius Sallow sitting, unaware of the baker's gaze. Patty's heart swelled with sadness as he watched Sebelius staring out the window, watching the morning breathe new life into what was supposed, for many, to be a magical day. Sebelius, harming no one now, just as he did in life, simply looked on and Patty felt a tear swell in his eyes.

"I am not a mean man. I never wish to make people feel less than they are, and I don't like speaking to people in the way you saw. I have no right to judge who is deserving of what in this life. We all enter and exit this world in the same way, but I will never fathom the injustice of why people like Sidney Betsy, and he isn't even the worst of our kind, navigate through life with very little problem, and the likes of you... well, end up like this," he said his piece and fell silent as he began to study the moving cityscape.

"I would have liked to have known you in life, Patty. I just thought I should let you know," Sebelius said, and, when he knew the words had landed, he turned back towards the shifting scenes that performed before his window.

"Well, it takes a special type of person, or spirit, to get me traipsing across town this early on a cold dark Christmas morning when I've had next to no sleep," Patty roared and went to place his hand on his shoulder, only for it to glide through. His heart sank even further, knowing he couldn't touch the most intangible being that caused him to feel so tangibly good inside.

Sebelius smiled sympathetically. "I am still getting used to it myself," he concluded. "Where did you go so early this morning when Mrs Perkins asked? I am intrigued, but tell me to keep my nose out of your affairs by all means."

"She knew very well where I had gone — to prepare the ovens. People still want bread on Christmas Day, and, when the bread is baked, the poor of our town bring along their meat, and I cook it for them." He broke off at a sight that stumbled wearily along the pavement, causing him to drop the window pane. Patty thumped once on the inside roof of the carriage to bring the horse to a trot and, leaning out, he hollered, "Merry Christmas, Perce! Still not home yet? Marlene will have your innards for a new stole," at the still inebriated Percy Trusett who wore a lady's gown in the Georgian style, stitched together with crimson fabric, and a bush of black hair that ominously perched on his head and looked in danger of becoming a beard.

"Ah, give us a lift, Pat," Percy shouted, "I think I might drop down dead before making it home, just for Marlene to kill me all over again."

"Sorry, my ol' mate, but I'm on an errand of mercy. Can't stop, and there's no way I'm paying for your fare back to Parson's Green."

"Where's your Christmas spirit, eh?" Percy lambasted.

"Why, Perce! He's in the cab with me right now!" He roared with laughter, giving two thumps to the ceiling so that they could resume their canter.

"Can you smell that, Sebelius?" Patty asked his companion, "Christmas is in the air."

"I can't smell a thing," Sebelius said. Patty's face failed to hide the disappointment at the thought of his friend's deprivation. "But I still have a heart, and although it doesn't beat, I can feel. I feel more now than I have ever felt before."

"Well, ain't that something," Patty acknowledged with subdued glee.

They disembarked in the square, Patty's attire causing curious looks from passersby as he handed his fare to the detestable Sidney

Betsy. Patty's hand remained suspended in mid-air until the appropriate change met his palm. He was renowned for being generous to a fault, and a "keep the change" rolled easily from his tongue, yet, when it came to some, he paid only for the services provided and not a farthing more. His broad knuckle rapped on the silky black front door of Aubrey Bravington's home, and, after a little time, it was opened.

"May I help you, sir?" the butler inquired, his eyes barely open at first, but widening upon analysing the caller. He pondered whether '*sir*' was indeed the correct term of address. A glance was exchanged between them, and the servant's fleecy eyebrows knit together in a frown.

Patty channelled the persona of his female character, infusing an air of refined manners and regal charm expectant of his ensemble, all the while subtly teasing the diligent valet in his execution of duties. "Is the master of the house present, my good man?"

"Ummm," the old valet's voice juddered through perplexity, giving Patty the impression that he was not long for this world himself, soon to be dragging his lonely spirit around London with him and his newfound friend. "Who shall I say is calling—" he broke off, trailing into silence.

"Who is it, Bethell?" a beautiful tone of female geniality rang out from within the hallway, which piqued Sebelius's interest.

"It appears," he cleared his throat, "to be Queen Elizabeth, your ladyship."

"Queen Elizabeth? What in the—" There, framed in the hallway, was a tall and arresting woman who stood as poised as an artist's muse, with a pale sharp face, hair perfectly fixed, and eyes that sparkled with inquisitive delight. "Goodness gracious, who in the devil are you?" the fresh-faced Lady Georgiana Grey inquired as she advanced to the door for a closer look. Sebelius found her appearance to be plainer than the accounts of her acclaimed beauty had suggested.

"Is Mr Bravington at home?" Patty asked once more.

"Please state your business? We were just about to open presents." Bravington's fiancée exclaimed, directing her attention from the visitor to address those in the next room. "Just a moment, Papa. There's some strange character at the door... No, remain seated, Papa. Goodness knows it took long enough to get you in the chair!" Lady Georgiana whimpered. "Kindly state your business," she demanded.

"I have been sent here with a message. I must deliver it in person. I have my orders, you see, m'lady."

"And from whom is your message?"

"Tell her," Sebelius consented.

"Sebelius Sallow, m'lady."

"Sallow? Sallow?" she said, biting the inside of her cheek, causing her lips to pucker and her eyes to roll back and forth as she thought about it. "I don't know such a fellow... wait... Sallow? Yes, that would be the little man that fixed Papa's watch before Christmas," she said gleefully.

Patty turned to look for further instruction from his companion and Sebelius nodded.

"Is there a problem? I trust he's been paid? I will inquire with my fiancé. Are you Mr Sallow's muscle, Mr—?"

Patty gave a perfunctory curtsy. "Stanley Perkins, m'lady."

"Well, if you are collecting debts on behalf of Mr Sallow — on Christmas Day — then you look positively terrifying in that costume, Mr Perkins." She laughed. "You really do look quite hideous, ridiculous even. Are you quite well? In the faculty department, I mean?" she said, tapping the side of her head with her finger. She continued, "Well, wait here, and I shall summon Mr Bravington, but don't keep him, you understand? We have church, so wait, you... wait... here!" She pointed to the spot on the ground where he stood in a most dominant fashion, as if scolding an animal, while Bethell stood guard. Her voice rang out, as she disappeared out of sight, that there was some lunatic at the door with a message from someone going by the name of Silas Swallow.

"I suspect we have lost m'lady in her excitement of Christmas. I will inform the master of your arrival," Bethell said and produced a salver for Patty's card, on which the baker placed his offering, causing the manservant's eyes to widen as he took it to the studio where his master pondered over his latest composition.

"A Mr Patty Cake to see you, Mr Bravington. He comes with a message from a Sebelius Sallow, sir," Bethell announced, proffering the silver tray holding one of Patty's famous, beautifully golden teacakes which Bravington lifted up and inspected with a sniff.

"Bring him to me, please, Bethell," he commanded, to which his faithful attendant dutifully obliged.

XII

Perched atop the enormous dome of St Paul's Cathedral, Sebelius quietened himself in the symphony of birdsong that serenaded Christmas morning. All of London was muted of its typical humdrum of urban clatter, amplified over the recent weeks by the preparations of the main event. His mind, caught in a relentless cycle, revisited the conversation he had witnessed between Patty Cake and the man who held his beating heart — when it did beat, that is — Aubrey Bravington. It was enough to descend him into despair.

It was the glimpse of a trampish-looking old lady, feeding her cooing and tweeting companions with meagre breadcrumbs, that triggered memories of Sebelius's beliefs. Bravington once suggested that the birds' morning chorus signalled to others of their species of their having survived the night, their jubilant voices singing to greet another day. Practical voices within Sebelius suggested simply that it was their form of communication, establishing territories and seeking potential mates, but his friend's romanticised notion overruled science.

It was during the Christmas holiday of that same year that thirteen-year-old Sebelius left school for home, brooding whether the same principle applied to his neighbours' chimneys. He pondered if the smoke signalled the houses that survived the night, and it was not merely the consequential residue of heat. This all began with the poignant memory of his neighbour, Mrs Simpson, and her dreadful passing, which reinforced his belief. It was her chimney's silence, contrary to its usual activity, that raised the alarm, marking an eerie stillness that hinted at more than just the absence of warmth.

His mind, as vibrant as that of any youth, fixated on matters far beyond his years. With his mother's sudden departure, an event of which he recalled very little, he vividly remembered the oppressive sense of sadness. This profound emotion was accompanied by an intense worry that one day, everyone dear to him might vanish as swiftly as a candle's light being snuffed out.

"Oh dear, you are in the doldrums," a sinister voice beside him articulated.

"Who's there?" Sebelius jerked with a start.

"You look as if you've lost eight pounds, fourteen shillings, and sev'npence and found yourself dead as the result of it," the man sneered, breaking into a hideous acrimonious cackle. "No, wait! There was a gold sovereign too, wasn't there?"

"Who speaks?" Sebelius demanded as the benefactor of the voice appeared next to him.

"Why, Sebelius, don't you know?" said the figure of a man with an amiable, cultured face, large-nose and mottled skin, with nose hair that transcended the nostrils and trailed down as an extension to his already sumptuous moustache. "You have reached rock bottom, and it is supposedly up to me to elevate you."

"So, which one are you?" Sebelius questioned.

"Greed, apparently," he said with something of defiance about the mouth.

"Yes," Sebelius agreed, acknowledging the spirit's astute observation. "I can see it." He cast a brief glance at the man, taking in his appearance before shifting his focus to more pressing matters, such as the captivating beauty of London's rooftops.

He, with his sapless chortle, which was his nearest approach to a laugh, asked, "Is it a crime, Sebelius, for a man to excel in business and covet all that he can, so he might secure not only his future, but his place in the world?"

"One supposes that depends upon whom you had to step on to obtain it, Sir Oliver," came the sweet, strong-minded tone of the most beautiful ethereal vision ever put to death and set to use, as her deadly sin namesake would have her. "The world and its desires pass away, but whoever does the will of good lives forever… so explain to us, what are you doing here exactly?"

Both Sebelius and Sir Oliver Doyle, who in life trod the gold-paved pavements and sidewalks of London and New York as an economist, financier, and banker, exploiting the economic potential of everyone and everything in his path, looked on at the blonde temptress in wonder. It was the Great Fire of New York City that was to be Sir Oliver's downfall.

Sir Oliver, whose salubrious privilege had always been to command and be obeyed, was now at risk of becoming the marionette.

"Who is that?" Sebelius muttered, as awe turned to admiration and hastily shifted to reverence at this feminine incantation of strength and desire.

"Lust," Greed said, as if even to say her name was laborious in itself, for everything became heavy under her spell.

"The very same, it's very nice to meet you Sebelius Sallow. Where is Charity, Greed? Not with you? Do not say that your unbridled avarice and insatiable appetite for wealth has seen him off?" Lust asked jocularly.

"Charity is working amongst the poor and destitute!" he replied in his brisk manner.

"Where is Chastity? Has she tired of your lascivious antics?" he mocked in return.

"Me? Little me? Tremendous little me. I am as sainted as they come," the seductress mocked, putting the palms of her hands together in prayer. Sebelius noticed that when she smiled all else ceased to move forward.

The horologist shook himself back to consciousness. "Without wishing to be impolite, could you perhaps take your disagreement elsewhere. I only wish to be alone."

Both Greed and Lust looked at one another. "Well, that's inconsiderate," Lust sneered and broke into a tuneful giggle. "Just admiring the view, are you? It is breathtaking, but I do not like height personally, well, not after my demise."

No words could ever narrate or do justice to Genevieve Milbrow, who stood tall, her golden locks cascading in defined curls that one could gladly spend an eternity separating one by one. Glacial eyes, plumptious lips painted a magnificent red, lashes as dark as coal, and a voice that could ensnare, beguile, and bewitch even Mother Nature. A native English noblewoman, her alluring exterior veiled a wicked deviousness, an unscrupulous, and, when necessity demanded, a ruthless interior. Her conquests were countless, her death... tragic. During her sojourn in France, her entanglement with the Comte de Deauville meant that fate, personified formidably as the Comtesse, his wife, cast her through the window of their chateau, imprinting a fear of heights upon her eternal soul.

"The view is splendid though, I must admit," she conceded, though she churned at the sight. "Don't look down, don't... look... down," Lust reminded herself. "You can do this, Genevieve. Goodness me, you can see the East End from here. You know, it is supposed that those in the East End utilise their copper to boil their brains throughout the year, only to replace them in their heads come December, making room for the pudding and all the other fare that will grace the family table. Imagine that?" Lust chuckled.

"Nonsense, dear heart," Greed interjected to quash the rumour. "This ridiculous piece of fiction was concocted by those in the West End, responding to claims from the East End that the culinary prowess in their kitchens lacked flavour. To address this, a stock is allegedly prepared by boiling toenails — strictly sourced from household members, as they are not heathens. Supposedly, this stock is the secret behind their renowned delicacies, imparting a distinct, albeit peculiar, note to their culinary creations. You see, it's all nonsense."

"No, I absolutely believe it. I have seen what they serve up there," Lust concurred, turning to her captivated companion. "So, Sebelius, are we ready to begin our adventure?"

"Now, wait a minute," the misanthropist squalled, his high, indignant voice resonating with remarkable malignancy. "This is not how it's supposed to be. Sebelius is melancholic beyond reproach, and that is where I excel!" He scowled with insensible fury.

The troubled spirit raised his slow, meditative eyes and, glancing at the intruding guests, wondered if he might finally attain the peace he had long desired. "At this point, Mr Greed, Madame Lust, I would gladly forfeit both of you," he announced heartlessly.

"I beg your pardon," Lust shrieked discordantly high, waving her hand up and down her incredible form in acknowledgement of her perfect proportions. "In a world where 'no' is a word, I am unaccustomed to hearing it. Think again, Sebelius Sallow. Greed is the spiritual representation of melancholy in the seven stages of grief. As for me, I represent the stage of upward turning, propelling you into stratospheres of spiritual growth." She said with a discreet smile that did not touch her voice. "You may stay here and wallow with him, or come with me."

"Come, Sebelius, plans of the diligent lead to profit," Greed applauded.

"As surely as haste leads to poverty," Lust jeered. "As long as it is day, I must do the work of him who sent me. Night is coming, when no one can work — and tonight this little lady has been invited to an enormous party, and it's quite a royal affair." Lust gave a pointed stare in Sebelius's direction, awaiting a decision. "Come, Sebelius. What do you say?" Lust whispered seductively in Sebelius's ear. "Do not tell me that you would pass me over for a man who uses his nostril hair in a bid to extend his moustache?"

"In truth, I don't know what to do... but what I am certain of is that I do not want to feel like this," Sebelius confessed, meeting the seductress's eyes then turning a fixed stare on Greed.

In a bid to secure her commission, the resplendent tease held out the luxuriant fabric of her dress, and Sebelius took it with limited hesitation.

"Then you have made your choice, and so you must stand by it.

Onto the next, one supposes," Greed conceded as he disappeared in the flurrying flock of flapping pigeons.

They sat a while as Sebelius regaled Lust of his past life and his rebirth in the afterlife, while she recounted events as the spirit of upward turn.

"Who decides? Well, my dear Sebelius, that is a very good question," Lust began. "Someone with a terrific sense of humour. Whoever put Sloth as the spirit of disbelief is beyond me, he lulls me to sleep, and Diligence resembles an overzealous governess — too much, too forceful. Envy, though technically not envious, is perfect as the spirit of pain and guilt but craves the adoration of any audience, even when there is none, while his husband, Gratitude, surprisingly turns out to be more tantalising than tedious. Wrath, now there's a peculiar fish; he is a natural for the anger stage that comes with grief, but he needs to breathe more, and fancy marrying his horse and all. Greed is, well, greedy, but his husband, Charity, is sweet — like a confectioner's window. He was a soldier in Philip of Spain's army. He was a defector, and a remarkably kind man. And then there's me, you know me, and what more perfect an embodiment of upward turn? Of course, there's Chastity, my wife. She took holy orders when she was alive. Well, they do say opposites attract, or maybe it's just celestial comedy at its finest."

"Is there anyone you *do* like?" Sebelius asked playfully.

"You, Sebelius Sallow. I mean, who couldn't?" She smiled, giving him a nudge of her shoulder.

"I feel less invisible now than I ever did when I was alive," he disclosed, which hit a cord within Lust that caused her to think.

She beckoned Sebelius to close his eyes, which he did reluctantly.

"I detest surprises."

"Oh! You cannot fail to like this one," she replied, enticing him to open them. In an instant, finding himself no longer seated upon the dome of the cathedral he was transported elsewhere — somewhere well known to him. For the first time since his passing, he believed he could smell, and it was the sweet, dusty, clag of bygone grandeur. It was the aroma of wooden furniture and the cold ironmongery that adorned it, the musky scent of aged books, the smoky whiff of leather and cloth binding them with glue, and the distinct redolence of tobacco and fires that warmed every corner.

The temptress took Sebelius's arm and they glided across the hall, her ample skirts swaying towards a door revealing a long, panel-clad, and somewhat stately corridor, with additional rooms branching off. She allowed him to lead the way, and they found themselves before a generous fire burning upon a spacious open hearth in a cosy gentlemen's retreat. Sebelius saw his younger self — seventeen years of age — reading his book, while his school friend, Aubrey Bravington, sketched intently in his pad. Whether Bravington was sketching or painting, he exhibited a graceful and swan-like approach, revealing little to no physical exertion. Yet, the speed and vigour of his activity upon paper or canvas mirrored the concealed, wild, flapping legs beneath the surface of the water.

"We spent hours like this, day after day, amid our studies," Sebelius reminisced. "Me in that chair and him always there. I would read, and he would sketch. I never wanted these moments to end. We were trapped in a place in time, where time did not exist."

"You forged a friendship here," acknowledged Lust.

"Indeed. We were eleven when we met. This is Christmas time, is it not?" Sebelius asked rhetorically. "Yes, it is." Sebelius smiled, a gesture more freely expressed now than ever before, as if, in life, this simple sign of emotion was stunted.

"What inspired him so greatly?" inquired Lust.

"I never knew; he would never show me. What artist wishes to share the ramblings of their mind put to life by their fingertips on paper?"

"Shall we take a sneaky peek?" she asked mischievously, gliding over for a look, which prompted Sebelius to call her away in a bid to maintain his friend's privacy. She held up a hand, and the memory for which they were only visiting, froze. "You do realise by now that these are only remnants of the past," Lust affirmed. "They will remain unchanged, and these fragments will remain oblivious to our existence. These are very good," she exclaimed with enthusiasm, flipping through Bravington's drawings in a manner that sufficiently piqued Sebelius's interest. "Wait!" she remonstrated as she concealed the paper against her chest, "What happened to maintaining his privacy?"

There was a swirl and spin of a mid-air chase, as both erupted into volcanic mirth, and Lust twirled forward as Sebelius pursued, encircling the panel-lined walls to the warmth at the top of the ceiling to the draughty rug-apparelled floorboards. With a swivel and a turn, Sebelius got hold of one of the sketches while the others discharged and flew like confetti suspended all around them. It was now he who was motionless.

"It's me," Sebelius observed, snatching at other examples for his consideration. "They are all of me." Sketches, studies, some detailed and some brief, but all were an exact likeness and each one captured the essence of his thoughtful gaze, the sharp cut of his side profile, his perfectly proportioned ears, his flawless skin, his distinctive nose and delicate mouth. They were undoubtedly all of him.

"Why did you part ways?" she asked thoughtfully.

"It's all a blur. This day was to be our last," Sebelius revealed, piecing together the events in his mind. "We left for our homes later that afternoon, for Christmas, and then... nothing. I wrote and wrote, but received no response. I even paid a visit to his home, which felt like a monumental obstacle. I was told he was not there, but I knew he was. They promised to relay my message, but no response came."

"I see..." Lust gave a wave of her hand, everything seemed to melt away.

The two young men, whose shared lives had become so intertwined that they were more like family than mere friends, had grown from apprehensive children into learned men. Each packed their belongings, their eyes averted throughout. They knew this would be the last time, and neither dared express the feelings they had for their friend. When Sebelius finally found himself unable to stop looking into Aubrey's unusually green, arresting eyes, he was moved to see they were clouded with unshed tears. Speechless, Sebelius felt waves of sadness wash over with great pain. He remained poised and stoic. It became all too real. He gazed unashamedly at the man who meant most to him in all the world, taking in his friend's delicate beauty. He vowed no matter where life took them, he would remember Aubrey Bravington forever. He also knew that the feelings he carried in his heart for the flame-haired youth could never be expressed, even if he had a lifetime.

The pair found themselves in the glorious entrance hall of the great mansion, which served not only as their place of education but their home. Both spirits observed the two young men, as they departed on their final day, ready to embark on their journey into the world in the new year. They were the last to leave.

"Goodbye, Sebelius. I hope, when we have settled back into our worlds beyond these sagacious walls, we will go on to be the best of friends in life, as we were here," the younger Bravington announced.

"I would like that… very much, Aub—" Sebelius's sentiment was stunted as he found that Bravington's lips pressed to his. The apparitions watched on as the two young men, concealed by an expansive partition of oak and stained glass, shared their first kiss in a blaze of colour. As their lips met, the two became one, embodying a bond that transcended names and identities, something more vast than their seventeen-year-old minds could fathom.

To Sebelius, there had always appeared to be a missing piece, to complete the broken picture in his mind. The final fragment fell into place when the erudite schoolmaster, Professor Buckleheath, saw their silhouettes in a thousand hues and vivid shades. The image not only displayed the parable of the Good Samaritan, but the birth of love between two people who could propel each other forward in a turbulent and cruel world.

In what he supposed was his great duty, Professor Buckleheath wrote a letter to Mr Bravington senior which put pay to any further involvement with his heir and the watchmaker's son.

All became clear.

XIII

"Sebelius Sallow, come down here at once!" the resonant voice of Patty Cake repeated as he stood, somewhat precariously, on the balustrade-lined balcony that encircled the foot of the dome.

"Who is that? Now there's the most interesting-looking chap I ever did see," Lust lusted. "Even beneath his skirts, you can tell he's a brute."

A shot look of disapproval came from Sebelius's direction at her lechery.

"Sebelius, we must go to Aubrey Bravington. He wants to help!" the baker yelled. "Can you please come down? I've just climbed a thousand and one steps to reach you, dressed like this. That is no mean feat." Patty sensed his friend's reluctance. "Please, Sebelius. It's Christmas Day, and I would like to get home sometime today or I'll be on the menu. Mrs Perkins will stuff me, baste me, and serve me with veg."

"Oh, there's a Mrs Perkins?" Lust muttered disappointedly to herself.

"How did you find me?" Sebelius crowed.

"Alfredo Rossi-Esposito-Santoro-Tassoni," Patty shouted.

"Who?"

"He is my spirit guide, well… of sorts. I inherited him from my mother, who is herself in the spirit world, but she refuses to talk to me, it's a very long story." He paused and pondered over the relevance. "Can we please get back on solid ground, and I'll explain?"

The lost soul found himself, once more, seated beside his burly friend in a hansom on their way back to the home of Aubrey Bravington, of whom Sebelius had thoughts he could not shake from his mind. Scenes of their carefree youth replayed, though Sebelius, always serious, couldn't quite embody carefree living. In life, he tried to imagine how his feelings for the artist would play out in society. Now, having gained the knowledge that his friend felt the same, the matter became even more complex. Would they have reunited to live as two bachelor men in lodgings, leaving the outside world to believe they were unfortunate in love, unlucky not to have found a lucky girl to capture their hearts? Impossible. London alone was riddled with marriages of convenience, with money or social elevation as the primary motives. Love seldom featured. Some were perhaps lucky to have it unfurl like flora in springtime, while others were like fungi, stagnated, in the dark, never flourishing too far away from where it existed.

The morning's encounter in Bravington's studio lingered heavily, resulting in Sebelius fleeing the scene and making for the comfort of St. Paul's and its heartening views of Ludgate Hill. It was the silence on their new journey that told Patty of Sebelius's unspeakable sadness. The changing morning light glinted upon Patty's solid features through the cab window, his brows furrowed by Sebelius's plight, and, though his strong lips parted to offer platitudes of hope, he found no words suited for the occasion.

"You should have been gentler with Aubrey when you delivered the news," Sebelius said, his eyes fixed on the window.

After a moment of contemplation, Patty responded. "I apologise, sincerely. It's difficult to become acquainted with someone such as yourself and not feel saddened by your plight. I believe Mr Bravington to be partly responsible for this," Patty offered his judgement.

"He's not, and you shouldn't think that," Sebelius absolved.

"If he had turned up yesterday—" Patty paused, feeling his emotions rising, and rethought his words. "It's what I believe to be true, whether you do or not, and that is for my conscience to bear."

Lust lay upon the roof of the two-wheeler as she amused herself with the carriage driver who was oblivious to her presence.

In the gentle motion of the carriage, Sebelius recalled Bravington's opening lines as he and Patty Cake entered the light, open, spacious studio for the first time that morning. "I can spare you only a few moments, Mr Cake, for we are soon away to church, there was some mention of my old school friend?"

Painted entirely in white, from ceiling to the boards that skirted the walls, the dark exposed oak floorboards were distinctly divided. One half was ablaze with colour from years of discarded paint, trodden in, while the other remained rich and unblemished. This detail clearly defined the artist's domain and that of any visiting parties.

"I won't take much of your time, Mr Bravington, but we do desperately need your help," Patty said humbly.

"We?" Bravington asked diligently, moving away from his easel.

The baker could see that the artist was an incredible, well-formed man, and that Sebelius's depiction of his imposing beauty was warranted. Despite his strong physique, his posture revealed the weight of considerable mental pressure. His pale complexion accentuated the flame of his hair and beard, and his solemn virescent eyes retained traces of the sparkle Sebelius had described — the lively essence that was his friend's usual demeanour. Patty could understand why this individual might effortlessly exude a captivating magnetism for those who graced his presence.

"I say we, but Sebelius Sallow, to be more exact."

"Sebelius? What about him? What is all this about, man?" he asked impatiently, as he moved to stand before his large visitor.

"Would you care to be seated, Mr Bravington?" Patty offered, his hand motioning to a model's chair.

"No, Mr Cake, I would not," he responded defiantly. "If you have come with a message from Sebelius Sallow then I will hear it."

"Sebelius Sallow is dead, Mr Bravington. I'm sorry to be so cold but you seem to be a man who, although artistic in temperament, likes his matters plain, and so there you have it."

Even Sebelius himself could not believe how callously Patty had delivered the news.

"ABut I?" Bravington responded in half voice. He repeated the outcome a second time, and it was then tears bubbled in his eyes. He stumbled back, and both Patty and his invisible friend lunged forward to grab him, but Bravington steadied himself against his artist's stool.

With pleading eyes, Sebelius urged his companion to go gently.

"I don't believe it, I can't believe it. I won't believe it." These mutterings of shock and disbelief kept bleating from the artist in his despair.

"It was the incident on the river that took him..." Patty announced gravely.

"The Thames tragedy? But... he would never... no... this is a nonsense." He sniggered at the ludicrousness. "Sebelius Sallow couldn't have been at the river. You have it all wrong."

Patty detailed all he knew of the matter, and of the boy he saved, the man that left him to die and the young girl who now travels with him in spirit. "He died bravely. I assure you, there is no nobler man I've been acquainted with than he. I've supped with dukes and street brawlers, esteemed and honest, wicked and reprehensible, and, of all these men, there was no finer."

Bravington jolted, rattled by disbelief. "I see, you are a charlatan."

"I will pardon you these wicked slurs, sir, because I know you to be grieving but if you were not I'd—"

Stepping before the increasingly angry baker, Sebelius instructed his large friend in how to deal with the matter a little more sensitively.

"He is instructing me to tell you that you saw him yesterday evening, at the shop, and again in the square—"

"All tricks of the light," Bravington admonished.

"Was it a trick of the light when you knew him to be in your chamber yesterday evening and you cowered like a little lamb, pleading him to leave because you could not bear to look on him again?" Patty snarled.

"I made quite merry yesterday evening with Earl Grey, and, in my slight inebriation I... wanted to see him. My mind showed me what I hoped to see." He paused and thought again of the ethereal figure he saw that bore the similarity of Sebelius Sallow. "It... it... was... terrifying... and not my Seb—" Bravington sighed as though it were his last breath. "It was not him."

Hearing these words, Patty witnessed Sebelius's torment and

Bravington demanded he leave his house.

"What are all these raised voices?" Lady Georgiana exclaimed as she marched in, unannounced.

"Your words wound him, sir," Patty scolded the artist. "He says, if you open your mind and you wholeheartedly wish to see him, he will show himself to you, right this instant."

"Who will? Don't say we are expecting more visitors, it's Christmas morning, we have church, followed by lunch with Mama and Papa," Bravington's fiancée bemoaned. "It's enough we have this imbecile man running amuck with that Simon Simple constantly on his lips."

"I am no imbecile, and his name is Sebelius Sallow!" Patty glowered at the affected noblewoman, which silenced her as she stood as referee between both men.

"Well, let's be having him," Bravington barked, clapping his hands as fear transformed into adrenaline. He appeared notably agitated, and his face quickly matched the florid hue of his hair. "Come on, Sebelius Sallow, I am all eyes and all ears, so I stand in wait."

The baker watched Sebelius and shifted his gaze to Bravington. His eyes bounced back and forth between their faces, anticipating the artist's expression of expectant fear, while the horologist appeared thoroughly beaten, hollow, aside from his spirited form, awaiting the impending disappointment he was likely to be faced with a third time.

"Well?" Bravington demanded, standing in wait.

"You cannot be trying," Patty returned.

"Oh believe me, Your Majesty, I am," Bravington barked at the baker.

"And you," Patty said, turning to his friend, "are you willing?"

Giving an unsure nod, Sebelius confirmed his part and they each waited.

"Oh! No! No! No! It can't be! There he is... is that him? He's terrifying! He's there!" came the screeching voice of one so petrified, so horror-stricken, her arm pointed at the void where Bravington gazed intently, yet where he could see nothing. Lady Georgiana's ankles buckled and gave way, bending to the knee, her hands remained outstretched upon the floor from where they broke her fall. She glanced up once more to confirm that her vivid imagination wasn't deceiving her, and it seemed that she might utter the word 'grotesque' before, upon inhaling, her eyes closed just moments prior to her cadaverous face meeting the floorboards with a whack.

"Does this perhaps help clarify the situation?" Patty said looking at the slumped mass of Lady Georgiana. "Shouldn't you see to your intended?" Patty pointed but Bravington stood transfixed, staring hard with a sincere desire to see his friend.

"I can feel you, Sebelius," Bravington said, so softly that it was more silence than a whisper. "Show yourself, please."

Patty called to his friend, yet it was clear that Sebelius had spirited himself away, and where better on Christmas Day than to St. Paul's?

"We're here," Lust announced as the hansom stopped in the little square outside Bravington's home.

"You didn't want him to see, did you? I understand that now," Patty acknowledged sensitively. "You shouldn't have vanished, either you want the help or you don't."

"I am beginning to scare myself," Sebelius confessed. "I wanted that absurd lady to see me, and I revealed myself as a thing so terrifying, that it might scare her half to death."

"Why would you do that?"

"Revenge?" Sebelius questioned aloud.

"You appeared as the same old Sebelius to me," Patty said and gave a reassuring smile.

"Being in my twenty-fifth year does not constitute as… never mind. It is because that's what I wanted you to see." His eyes fell regretfully.

"There is nothing we can do about it now. After Lady Grey was put to her bed, me and your chap devised a way we can help you, your mother, and Laidey, but you must comply, Sebelius, or all is lost." And so Patty went on to explain the plan.

"Mr Patty Cake to see you once more, sir," Bethell announced, leading Patty into a small study, followed by Sebelius and Lust. Lust made a grand entrance, creating an enormous hoo-ha about the delectable Aubrey Bravington, who rose from behind his desk to greet the baker and his unseen companions.

"I can feel his presence," Bravington declared, but Patty, about to acknowledge this, found his concentration marred by Lust's noisy excitement over the dashing artist. This display naturally piqued Bravington's curiosity, prompting Patty to quash it immediately with a stern remonstrance, aiming to avoid further distraction or delay.

"Where do you want me?" the artist inquired.

"Seated would be safer," Patty instructed, drawing from the knowledge of his mother, who possessed a far greater gift than him in such matters and had seen this done many times before.

"What is going on here?" Lust questioned.

"You'll see," Patty replied, "but we will need absolute silence. If that will be a problem for you, please leave." To which Lust glided her finger across her lips to indicate that they were now sealed. "Now, Mr Bravington, although you are a willing participant there will be some resistance from you. It is natural as your body will fight against any threat of invasion, but you must allow it to happen."

With all in place, the ritual commenced. Patty's words guided their actions: eyes closed, palms flat on the table with fingers spread wide, breaths syncopated with the acceptance of positivity on the inhale and the purging of negativity on the exhale. A trance settled over the room as Sebelius stepped forward, taking his place behind his friend and resting his hands upon his shoulders. In the privacy of Bravington's mind, a profound response was visible as Sebelius heard, "I can feel you, Sebelius." Fingers glided down the artist's strong arms, and hands ran over the tops of his. Sebelius's spirit gently infiltrated Aubrey Bravington's mortal body, and, true to form, the artist writhed and flailed in his seat. The crimson hairs rose along the line of his neck, igniting a sensation that made his eyes bulge and his mouth gape downward, as though his tongue had rolled out onto his lap. Amidst the inner turmoil, an urge to scream emerged, yet he found himself only capable of emitting a hoarse croak, distant and detached, as if his own voice bellowed from another room.

"Acceptance serves as the key to unfasten the door to any adversity that might have bolted it," Patty's voice boomed, and the artist fully submitted, leaving Sebelius once more weighted in the gravity of Aubrey Bravington's skin. With a sharp inhale of breath, the first since his life was extinguished on the frigid Thames, his eyes sprang open, greeted by Patty leaning over the desk, gripping him by the wrists.

"Breathe, good lad. Are you quite well?" Patty asked.

"I wouldn't say quite well. I am still dead." Sebelius smirked, revealing his friend's set of perfectly white teeth.

"And Mr Bravington?"

"He is with me, but languid, you might say." With those words, Sebelius absorbed a lifetime of thoughts and feelings from his friend — joyous, jubilant, godforsaken, and desolate. The pain of experiencing these emotions was crushing, especially as they were not his own, and if he could have stripped away the pain of his friend's suffering, leaving only the elation of joy, he would have gladly done it. "I am ready to begin," Sebelius instructed.

Patty presented before him a substantial amount of exquisitely fine paper, lined envelopes, a quill, and a silver inkwell. With earnest intent, Sebelius began to write in the room's silence. The only sounds to be heard were the scratching of the nib on paper as words flowed naturally, and the hissing and spitting of the fire on the hearth, like a pit of angry vipers.

"My last will and testament," Sebelius declared firmly, extending the quill for Patty to witness, backdating the document to the seventeenth day of December, Sebelius's birthday. All documents were duly verified with this date, and in doing so, Sebelius supported a new belief that there should be nothing unnatural about putting one's affairs in order on the anniversary of one's birth. Mortality becomes a highly conscious subject upon the day we enter the world, and there is comfort in making peace with the preparations that we will one day have to depart it.

"Your handwriting is a thing of beauty," Patty declared as he folded it and stuffed it into the envelope. Sebelius, however, was already onto the next, causing the baker to smile.

"For the undertaker," Sebelius said, waving the paper under his makeshift secretary's nose, ensuring it too would be folded and stuffed. Patty did as he was instructed without words or defiance. "For my mother," he declared after penning his sentiments. "For Aubrey," he handed the document to the baker, who took it but was interrupted in his task as Sebelius gripped Patty by his meaty wrist, instructing, "Not to be given to him until I am laid to rest. Promise me."

"Have I ever let you down?" the burly man declared, to which no answer was given nor required. "Are we all done? It is best not to delay these matters. This will be taking its toll on Mr Bravington."

His task complete, Sebelius rose from the desk, the mass of flesh and bone slumped forward in his seat. The floodgates of Bravington's locked heart were opened; the man, overpowered by the weight of his love and grief, hid his face as he sobbed passionate tears on the blotting pad where his head lay.

"I think I should perhaps leave you for a moment," Patty said respectfully, moving into the hallway, leaving the anguished man to mourn his devastating loss.

XIV

The door closed to the Westminster home, leaving Bravington and Patty on the pavement of Smith's Square, each resolute in their task to resolve the affairs of their mutual friend, Sebelius Sallow.

"Are we all clear?" Patty began, prompting Bravington to pat the breast of his frock coat where the papers lay beneath. "Sebelius, summon your father and Laidey to the hospital. Lust, make your way to that place now. As for Mr Bravington and myself, we shall share a cab."

They agreed to their assigned roles, and, as Bravington hailed a cab preparing to depart from the square, he uttered, "Godspeed, Sebelius. We will make this right."

"How are you feeling?" Patty inquired of the apparition, whose spirits had been lifted having been reunited with his old friend, despite Sebelius being on the opposite side of their unchosen divide.

"Relieved. I would have to agree that the working-through stage has begun," Sebelius answered cheerfully. "I forgot the joys of putting pen to paper."

Bravington called out to Patty through the open door as he settled into his seat, and instructions of their journey were conveyed to the driver as the baker's skirts swept the pavement in its direction.

"Uh oh, you should not have said that," Lust said regretfully. "New stage, new spirit," she uttered woefully as a hansom from the spirit world, the driver appearing a little worse for wear from alcohol and the subsequent demise, pulled up before them. "Prey, you jest with me?"

"What is it?"

"Your new incarnation, Sebelius. The next time someone asks you if you're well, say something in the vein of, 'I'm keeping my spirits up.'" His confidante spoke these words in jest, yet they were shrouded with grave disappointment. "Officially, I am now to move on," she said in her calculating tone. In life, Lust's governess had warned her that strong emotions ruined not only one's appetite and complexion, but one's rouge, so she never ran to it even in her spiritual form. She refused to become the wailing banshee of nightmares, though the thought amused her.

"But you can't, you mustn't, we need you," he pleaded.

"Oh! You are a sweet boy but I do not make the rules—"

"Forget all your doubts, for Pride is hereabouts," said the sixth of his order as he alighted the carriage. "Hullo, you dear, dear man," he said, taking Sebelius by the elbow. "Lusty. How are you?" the gentleman of a remarkably debonair persuasion greeted the temptress.

"Sebelius, this is Pride. He came before my fall. Do you remember, Colonel?" Lust grinned.

"Colonel?" Sebelius returned, pensively.

"Colonel Thomas Pride of—" Lust began to formalise their introduction, but none was required on Sebelius's part.

"Oliver Cromwell's New Model Army. You were one of our

subjects in school, sir," Sebelius said, quite taken with the infamous soldier. It wasn't that he was particularly enamoured with war or notoriety, but, as a topic taught to all true Britons, he was fascinated by the one spirit he knew, aside from his father.

"Stuff and nonsense, we are all equal here, though I believe great things are destined for you, young Sebelius. Let us depart and work our way through this penultimate stage so we can set you on your way to acceptance. It is through acceptance that great things happen," Pride said and Sebelius believed him. How could he not?

Towering with arms akimbo, he was a man of tremendous stature and the prominence of his husky frame was beautified by an intricately quilted and embroidered doublet. His face was a striking triangle sculpted by prominent cheekbones, a sharply groomed golden moustache, and a pointed cone-shaped chin beard. All these attributes were neatly mounted by swathes of ashy-blonde hair.

"I think not," Lust protested. "This young man is still on the upward turn, and is nowhere near ready. Besides this is the most fun I've had in several other people's lifetimes and you're not usurping me now. I am a much more formidable opponent than King Charles ever was. Do you wish to put me to the test?"

Colonel Pride teased his golden beard dubiously and looked from one to the other of the younger spirits in mild agitation. "Shouldn't we join forces?" he proposed. A gratified smile spread across his face which was to reward him many a successful conquest.

"We most certainly should not!" she replied without hesitation.

"Wouldn't our endeavours be strengthened with as many bodies — apologies, spirits — assisting us as possible?" Sebelius corrected himself.

"Well…" Lust began, but Sebelius interrupted her.

"Lady Milbrow," he addressed her, affecting a small bow. "You, who art the supreme spiritual embodiment of the great capital vice and cardinal sin known to all as lust, know this, I could not and would not wish to continue this journey without you. You will stay, and afterwards we shall always be the greatest of friends. But let's accept help where it's offered. Agreed?" His words stirred her emotions, causing them to rise and bulge in her throat and eyes.

"Agreed," Lust said gratefully. "Additionally, I am not a lady, just a miss."

"To me, you are," Sebelius responded in a charmingly reverent manner.

"My dear Sebelius, I do believe your sense of humour is improving," she announced proudly.

"Well, I have you to thank. Now, can we please depart from here?" he requested with some urgency. "You two must go to the hospital and I shall find my father and the little one."

"Come along, Thomas," she commanded, seizing the hand of the soldier and bundling him and herself into the ethereal carriage before shutting the door. "Well, you didn't mention you brought your wife along," Lust exclaimed, concealing her disgruntlement as the carriage began to hasten, prompting a smile from Sebelius. "How are you, Humility dear? I adore what you're wearing. You must introduce me to your dressmaker. Please don't break my heart and tell me he is still alive?"

Closing his eyes, Sebelius envisioned a place he wished to visit and the faces he longed to see, knowing that there he would be.

Mr Cannadine was nestled beside his fire, anticipating the hearty measure of brandy about to quench his palate, when the five resolute knocks of Bravington's silver ball-handled cane against the glossy black door jolted the proprietor from his fancy. The undertaker, known for his patience, cast a disapproving glance mid-air, contemplating the consequences of his inaction. However, a further five raps caused him to set his glass down, duty compelling him to answer the summons.

"Season's greetings, good sir," murmured the undertaker of Cannadine and Smidge, in a drawl that was never to extend beyond its one note. "Please, come in and tell us how we may assist you?"

The artist apologised profusely for intruding, acknowledging the sanctity of the day. The tall, thin, grey-faced man, with his long, thin nose, grizzled hair, whiskers, and large, wide watery eyes, absolved him with a thin-lipped remark about death's utter disregard for the time of year or festivities. This immediately put Bravington at ease, although the imposing, sombre atmosphere of death did not. To himself, Mr Cannadine often boasted that business could never be considered limited in its clientele, for death never ceased. Having laid to rest the recently mourned King William and his royal predecessors, his firm was expected to do the same for Queen Victoria when that time came. His enterprise was highly sought after.

"We operate every day, being the largest and oldest funeral director in London." Mr Cannadine concluded, and Bravington explained.

"The Thames tragedy, I see. You are correct that we were given the responsibility of preparing the departed of that awful occurrence for their final destination in this life. It is your friend, you say, that you believe passed in the incident?"

The flame-haired man discreetly steadied himself against the onslaught of emotions threatening to overpower him. It was a struggle that on the surface might have appeared unnoticed or perhaps mistaken for mild agitation, but he feared its effects were far too visible. The artist held back the tears that threatened to cascade like an unyielding waterfall. The harsh, vile words spewing out from beyond the safety of his mind which threatened to be fired at anyone who looked at him disapprovingly, and the pain in his gut felt like a pack of hounds tearing at the spoils of his innards. Grief was never set to be pretty, which brought the bearer the hideous mask of contorted features, all topped off by a runny nose.

"In your own time, Mr Bravington," the official said patiently.

"My friend," Bravington paused, pondering the word 'friend' and considering what other socially acceptable term could encapsulate the depth of his feelings which consumed every part of his being. "Sebelius Sallow, is around six feet, his hair the golden colour of buttered toast, his skin pale and flawless, his nose long, straight and proud, lips that have never uttered a curse against a living soul, and a chin in the shape of a delicate heart."

Mr Cannadine coughed dryly into his fist. "I know the very gentleman, sir. Mr Sallow is ready to receive you," he replied stiffly, but even the suave undertaker could not fail to be moved by such a beautiful characterisation of someone so dear. "Given the circumstances of the tragedy and the time of year, my assistants have worked through the night so that all are ready for Christmas Day."

For just a matter of minutes, Bravington stood in the small sitting room, warmed by the welcoming glow within a heavily ornate fireplace, before being summoned by Mr Cannadine into a room at the end of the tastefully furnished hallway.

The artist paused at the threshold of the open door, feet

anchored to the floor, for this was finality at its most absolute.

"There is nothing to fear, sir. He wouldn't hurt you in life and so would not do so in death," Mr Cannadine reassured him as he looked in. Bravington's focus rested upon the wooden vessel, perfectly lit and perfectly centred within a perfectly charming room. But it wasn't fear of Sebelius Sallow's mortal remains that gripped him; it was the confirmation of his permanent loss and the realisation that, from this moment on, life would never be the same again. He would have to endure each day until the end of his natural time without Sebelius. Despite the years of separation, he had thought of his friend every day, finding comfort and reassurance in the belief that they would always be under the same sky, in the same city. He lived with the hope that their paths might cross again, with the possibility of rekindling their friendship. He was suffocated by a mental fog, thicker than any notorious dung-tainted London peasouper. However, it was the intensity of sorrow that blinded his vision, filled his lungs, and clung to the fabric of his clothes, or it might have been the cloying scent of sentimentality and the mournful pollen permeating the air. In this haze, everything was a blur, but his consciousness remained aware of the reassuring click of the door closing with Mr Cannadine on the other side. He couldn't divert his eyes from the one thing he could never imagine growing bored of. 'Angelic', the word pushed through the murkiness of Bravington's mind as his gaze brushed over Sebelius's pronounced features as delicately as someone brushing a feather along the skin with the gentlest of touches. Angelic? He thought again and instantly chastised himself for reducing this precious being to such a cliché.

The profound internal disquiet and overwhelming emotion

that results after allowing a recently departed soul entry into your own body so that they might fulfil their final wishes are beyond imagination. Bravington, too, found himself unprepared for the depth of this experience, as its effects lingered within him like an unwelcome guest. Gripping the edge of the unbefitting, yet expertly crafted coffin made of pine, his fingers squeezed so tightly that he cared little if his bones might splinter through his white flesh.

Reflecting on his experience when the trance-like state began, and he had surrendered himself to Sebelius's soul, he remembered the murky white cloud swirling before his eyes, morphing into shades of grey and then swiftly to black. The paralysis of his soul was its surrender and, in the cloudy mist, his displaced spirit settled as Sebelius seized control, absorbing, without intention, every sensory experience he had ever known since birth. Yet he was wholly unprepared to be immersed in all that Sebelius had encountered in his past too.

Attempting to silence the demented notion of the narratives of two lifetimes in one mind, he inwardly shut himself off, akin to a child who plugs its ears and hums loudly and squawks to drown out unwanted noise. Yet, despite his efforts, the chaos persisted elsewhere, as the human body's organs tirelessly worked. The intricately connected networks that move air, fluids, solids, and all other substances in between continued. So much noise, so much activity. That system of nerves, the responders of pain, the intricate movements of joints supported by muscles, sinews, and fibres — all contributing to noise — like a ship yard in full vigour. Yet outside there is silence, an eerie quiet of indifference as the meaty flesh of human existence insulates the deafening sounds within.

Pulling one of the two chairs positioned against the wall, each side of an ornate oak sideboard, the artist settled beside his friend and gazed at his face intently, committing every detail to memory, knowing it would be the last time he would see it. In an unconscious act, he began to hum the tuneful melody that was synonymous with them both. As always, it filled the silence but this time it played a greater role in steadying his heart, suppressing tears, and reminding him of his love.

XV

In contrast, it took only three resounding thumps on the large lilac stained-glass door of the Bayswater residence for Patty's summons to be answered. He found himself face to face with a disproportionately large houseboy, who regarded him with evident confusion.

"The mistress of the house, if you please!" Patty delivered in a deep, gruff tone, more of a command than a request.

The bulging youth, gulping down his perplexity at seeing a towering female impersonator, analysed him with flickering, anxious eyes and produced a silver salver expectantly.

"There ain't no time for all that. I come on an errand of great mercy. Tell your mistress that Sebelius Sallow sent me."

Instantly, upon uttering these words, Patty was ushered into an auspicious drawing room where he stood at its centre like a queen awaiting her audience, turning smoothly to take in the room's grandeur. Beautiful silk wallpaper, adorned with resplendent flowers, surrounded him. Heavy furniture crafted from the darkest wood bore a lifetime of trinkets and treasures, and rococo frames held ancestors preserved in oil. Patty couldn't help but wonder why some, who looked as they did, might wish to be eternalised forever in memory by the artist's brush.

The door swung open, revealing a figure who wasn't the person Patty had requested, but rather her husband. Colonel Cecil-Yule's black eyes were restless, crafty, and cunning; his mouth and chin agitated in a motion as if he were sucking a humbug, though he wasn't — it was the vexation of his unexpected and unwelcome visitor, especially upon hearing the name Sebelius Sallow, which shaped his mouth. His complexion was hard, the kind that never looked content or wholesome.

"What do you mean by coming here?" Colonel Cecil-Yule demanded sharply.

"I did not darken your door to see you, but your wife," Patty retorted, with the obvious absence of the usual courtesies such as 'sir' or an apologetic tone.

"My wife?" he scolded loudly, as if he were addressing a regiment of men. "Do you think it's acceptable for a man to call at a respectable residence and request an audience with another man's wife? Do you, man?" He paused, eyeing Patty's regal attire. "I trust you are a man?"

"Oh, believe me, I'm a man alright," Patty replied vehemently. If his features didn't convey the intensity of his tone, the swelling of his hairy arms and fists certainly did. The commander noticed, and his brows raised in response. "Now go get your wife, for I'm not leaving here until I've seen the lady of the house."

From the dark wooden side table, gleaming with a mirror finish, the tactical leader retrieved a small bell and rang it, summoning the same disproportionate servant.

"Bring my wife!" he scowled. Within moments, Sebelius Sallow's mother entered the room, offering a cursory bow of her head to the visitor, followed by curious glances.

"You wish to see me, sir?" Euphemia Cecil-Yule queried, shifting her eyes towards her husband for some level of response. The military officer, still agitated, prepared for his departure.

"Don't go on my account, Colonel Cecil-Yule, this concerns you too," Patty instructed, hindering his retreat. "I come at the behest of your son, Mrs Cecil-Yule."

"Sebelius?!" she exclaimed.

"The very same," Patty confirmed.

"I fear there is some mistake. My son does not know of my existence, or at least of my living existence." She paused, realising she was wasting time on unimportant matters. "What news of my son?"

"I have been asked to deliver this into your hand," Patty said, withdrawing a long powder-blue envelope and placing it delicately in her hand.

It took one purposeful swipe for the letter knife to reveal the contents within and Effie's eyes traced over her son's beautifully formed handwriting.

It ran thus:

Mama,

I start by writing that I know, at last, all that is needed to be known. I do not write these words with the bile of bitterness or spite of sorrow, but the unction of understanding.

In the stillness of this snowy December day, marking my twenty-fifth year, I do not celebrate, as the term 'celebration' and all the things that come naturally to the occasion, have never quite come naturally to me.

Though to express emotion has been a stumbling block,

life's capricious turns have, in their own way, unveiled layers of my being, shedding light on who I once was and guiding the path for who I shall become.

Father's unexpected passing in the spring revealed a truth that is now very clear to me. He chose not to publish announcements of his death, as he wished to shield me from shattering the illusion of your own passing, but I know this was a lie of his creation in order to protect me from the feelings of inadequacy that come from abandonment.

I hope the life you have built with the man you chose over your family has truly brought you happiness. While your absence was felt, perhaps less so had I known the truth, gain comfort in knowing that days spent with Father, where laughter, joy, and love flowed freely, made me feel truly comfortable in myself and always wanted.

In the eventuality of any misfortune befalling me on my journey forward, I pen this to declare that all I possess shall be solely yours. No claims should be made by your husband, as often transpires in such situations.

If, by an unnatural order, where a mother should outlive her child, I extend my wish for your happiness in the years to come — a happiness akin to the one Father and I shared, where he cared and reassured me until his final breath.

Your ever-existing son,
Sebelius

Her eyes flooded with emotion as her gaze moved up and then back down to the words. She never expected to receive a pardon for her inadequacies as a mother or for foolishly following her heart.

Although Sebelius and his father had a place in that aforementioned heart, it never presented itself as strongly as her love for Joshua Cecil-Yule. She traded the name Sallow for Cecil-Yule for what she believed was true love, but to truly understand and appreciate love, one must be able to discern between reality and fantasy, and not be swayed by impulsive or irrational emotions.

"I wish to see him," she said in a strong voice. "I need to see my son. Will you take me to him, Mr...?"

"Perkins, madam. Stanley Perkins," he spoke, proposing to continue swiftly, thus sparing the woman the pains of speaking in her optimistic fashion. However, she interrupted the messenger before he could proceed.

"Mr Perkins, thank you. God bless you for bringing me such news. This is truly the greatest Christmas gift I have received since the first, twenty-five years ago. I will get my cloak, and we will be away."

"No, madam. I'm afraid it is not quite that simple."

Her look of gratitude turned quickly to anger, then defiance. Although Sebelius knew nothing of her existence, his mother knew of his. At certain times, she would stand on the adjacent pavement, lost in the bustling crowd, and watch her son at work through the window. She longed for the courage to cross the road and make his acquaintance, but she knew it would shatter his world and bring destruction to hers at home.

"I will save you the trip, madam. Your son is dead. Apologies for being so brusque, but I speak plainly," Patty declared, allowing his words to sink in. "He perished in the Thames tragedy yesterday evening." His report rang as woeful as a church bell and with the same weight, as it brought the lady crashing down onto her chair.

Her husband remained unmoved, with not even a flinch in her direction.

With this news, Colonel Cecil-Yule's expression turned grotesque. A ghastly smile appeared on his granite features, seemingly the result of habitual malice, giving him the aspect of an alligator in wait, but it was not to last.

"That letter is his final say on the matter. It's a good job he wrote it and learned about you at the last, because his death has gone unnoticed by all, save me and his friend, Mr Aubrey Bravington. The Government would have gladly seized his property as their own, and by the time you had learned of it, it would have been too late. I dare say you might not have claimed your inheritance for fear of it going to him," Patty continued insolently, nodding his head in the commander's direction as he spoke. "At least now, madam, this letter grants you all that is left — the shop, the house, and assets. I'm assured it is a not-too-inconsiderable sum." Patty's tone changed from counsellor to that of a dictator. "You can start over, madam. You will make a better life, that is unless blissful happiness detains you here, though I suspect it does not."

Their visitor made his way towards the exit, and Colonel Cecil-Yule reached for the handle just as the door swung inward in his direction.

"The funeral is arranged by his friend, whom I've mentioned, and you shall receive your summons when details are put into print, madam. I suspect your husband may be otherwise engaged on that day," Patty said presumptively, preparing his departure into the hallway, and yet he stopped at the door. Patty Cake dropped his eyes to the commander's shoes with a disdainful smirk, then slowly lifted his gaze from them to his ankles, progressing upward to his shin, then his knee, and onward in a deliberate manner, all the while extending up the inner of his legs. His scrutiny continued, ascending from the waistcoat, button by button, until it reached the chin. Following a straight path up the centre of the nose, he finally arrived at the eyes, and with a suddenness, he declared, "I have feasted upon greater men than you while waiting for Mrs Perkins to plonk my mains on the table."

Now Patty was ready to take his leave. He brushed past the imposing footman and stepped out into the embrace of the sweet, invigorating winter air. The street, though still bare of the usual bustle, was littered with a handful of passersby; they traipsed from house to house of their kith and kin, exchanging season's greetings, their only incentive being the promise of a glass of Christmas cheer and the company of kindred spirits.

"Will these vagrants and layabouts not drag themselves to some other quarter and clutter up the pavements and doorways there?" admonished a passing gentleman to his intended, who pointed his cane at a destitute man slumped nearby, whose name had long since shrivelled up and died. He was to be known henceforth as a mere drifter, wanderer, rover... vagabond.

"Who would miss them if they were to die where they lay?" she responded with her usual air of superiority.

Their rancorous bile could hardly go unnoticed by Patty or the subject of their observations.

"Here you go, Dad," Patty said to the destitute man, placing a few pennies in his hand. This man was not Patty's father, but he was paying homage to his age and a respect that he could be anyone's father.

"God bless you for a gentleman. One with a sense of humour at that," the man replied, recognising his benefactor's style of dress. "It's life that did this to me, sir, to all of us. Our homes are wherever we may find rest. What you heard is not the worst of what's been said. We settle down like animals in doorways or quiet corners, and on a day like today, it's even worse. But I think of our Lord today, especially, but I can only mark the occasion as if the day were like any other. It's the silence that kills on a day such as this, the inactivity only amplifies our misery. We are the people who all turn away from, seeking more cheerful distractions, as if our plight isn't happening all around them. The truth is, my son, it could be any one of us. The only difference between us and folk like them is luck. And so we trudge on, and they remain deaf to our calls for charity."

A few pennies more were placed in the old man's hand and steadying the man to his feet, Patty instructed, "Get yourself a cab to the Lamb and Flag, Covent Garden. Tell Mrs Perkins that Patty sent you, and a Christmas feast awaits you. Please tell her that I'll be home soon."

This act came as a lesson learned very early in life and instructed by his mother that, "If we do nothing when we can reach out and help when we see those in the depths of suffering, remorse is a hollow thing when mercy arrives too late to bring any comfort."

The baker's swift attention to other pressing matters was hindered by the distracting wheeze of breathlessness creeping up from behind him — a sound unmistakably belonging to one being, his spirit guide, Alfredo Rossi-Esposito-Santoro-Tassoni, adopted from his mother's passing into the afterlife.

"Does my mother send you?" Patty inquired, and each time he hoped that he might answer in the affirmative.

"No, signore," the spirit guide wheezed. "She still no speak to you. I come to tell you that Sebelius Sallow needs most urgently to speak to you," he concluded between fits of coughing.

The ghoulish spirit, once Italian in life, bore the remnants of his mortal existence. He wore a large-rimmed, high-pointed hat reminiscent of old witches from folklore, and his long white hair hung in fine, scraggly folds beneath it. His attire consisted of worn hessian rags fashioned into robes and pointed, capacious shoes. His hands, coarse and dirty, had thin, warlock-like fingers that resembled claws more than hands, with irregular, long, brown fingernails that extended them further.

"Then we are to be on our way," Patty instructed, while his otherworldly guide updated the clairvoyant on the topic of his summons as they journeyed through the cobblestone streets that were embroidered in thick ice.

XVI

The Westminster Hospital, is a forsaken institution where the frightened and vulnerable gather in their time of need, bound not by choice but by the inexorable constraints of their mortal existence. Bereft and forsaken, they find themselves entrusted to the care of strangers amidst their greatest trials and tribulations. Though no hands, however gentle, could ever replace those of a mother, father, wife, husband or child, the unfamiliar touch of nurses attending to unfamiliar patients somehow manages to provide comfort and compassion. In the simple act of wiping a fevered brow or soothing the confusion of senility — where the absent-minded call out for the love of a mother, long since passed, yet believed to be nearby — these caregivers offer a semblance of reassurance and care, even when there is none. In the selfless dedication of these nurses, tirelessly tending to the needs of the afflicted, there lies a generosity of spirit that transcends monetary reward.

Led by his ever-present Italian spirit guide, Patty Cake found himself greeted by a gathering of anxious souls awaiting his arrival. They were in none other than the Bravington Ward, a name bestowed by the senior gentleman of his name. His dedication, boundless wealth, and remarkable capacity for empathy towards those beyond the confines of his family, distinguished him. While not inherently cruel or unkind, it was a profound sense of gratitude from strangers that propelled him forward, rather than any pride his family, especially his son, Aubrey, might have harboured.

"Patty! I apologise for the summons, but we didn't know what else to do," Sebelius blurted anxiously.

"Sebelius, breathe. Well, not that you can actually breathe, but stay calm," Patty interjected, exhaling deeply. "Continue."

"Laidey's mother has been found," Sebelius continued. "There she lies, unresponsive. We didn't know what to do. No one will acknowledge us."

"It is because you are all dead," the baker expressed jocularly, peering down the rows of beds on either side, where his eyes remained permanently fixed on the last one.

"You must take care not to get struck down wearing that attire, or you shall wear it for all eternity," Sebelius returned, a prophetic curse but it was delivered in jest.

The ward was a bleak house of sickness. The deep, frigid blue sky, unblemished by a single cloud yet ablaze with brilliant light, failed to uplift the foreboding aura of the place. Despite its efforts to illuminate the ward, the dim glow of lamps remained necessary amidst the austere atmosphere. Here, the sombre dullness of the surroundings mirrored the struggles of those in the grip of sleep, pain, and on the cusp of eternal rest. Countless individuals grappled with affliction and indisposition, tempering even the most sprightly of creatures, in disjointed ramblings of absent minds, groans of suffering, and whispered prayers from lips soon to be silenced by the grave.

Taking gentle steps, Patty traversed the ward, casting glances with a half-awkward smile, as if hoping to alleviate their suffering or seeking forgiveness for daring to look upon them in their most wretched and downcast state. In one bed lay a young child, rendered unconscious by his pain; his face, arms, and chest a vivid pink and raw from the scalding effects of boiling water. He lay perfectly still, his flesh seeming to writhe of its own accord, such was the extent of his misery. Ointments and non-adherent gauzes were applied with the absolute attentiveness. In the next bed lay a little old woman, mutilated by an affliction in her forgetfulness, thrashing her limbs against the scant mattress requiring the intervention of three good strong men to prevent further harm. Further along, a young boy lay motionless and solitary, deprived of family by his bedside, seemingly deep in the clutches of the worrisome oblivion of healing slumber, which bore an uncanny resemblance to the moments preceding death.

At the far end of the room lay the focal point of Sebelius's concern and Laidey's grief — a young woman with delicate features, scarcely twenty-five years of age. Her once lustrous brown locks now lay limp and matted upon her pillow, streaked with clumps of blood from the cuts and bruises inflicted during the cruel assault of the Thames and the frantic efforts of her rescue. Though her pretty face remained largely unmarred save for bruises, it was rendered even more pallid by the lifeless shade of white that had overtaken her complexion since being pulled from the water. Her limp arms, which had valiantly fought against the icy currents, now lay at her sides, adorned with a multitude of purple blotches, souvenirs of the brave hands that had grappled to save her.

"Laidey, this is the friend I spoke of, this is Patty Cake," Sebelius introduced with a gentle smile, addressing the little child curled upon her mother's bed.

However, she remained still and Patty Cake's attention soon drifted elsewhere.

He turned to the passing head of the ward, who wore her position and name upon her breast, Matron Wraithpaugh. "What is the current status of this woman? I must know."

She was a paunchy woman, her irritation so well practised, it was a fine art. She chose not to acknowledge Patty's open-hearted concern for a patient in her charge, presumed abandoned by all without a care in the world. Instead, she gave him the customary once-over, performed with the accomplished precision only someone in her position could muster. With a sigh of indignation, she inquired, "Are you a relative? Many of those rescued from the Thames have been claimed, except for waifs and wastrels."

"I suppose, I'm a family friend… though family is a loose term. She has no one left, her child perished tragically in the incident," Patty replied solemnly.

"Then, as you are no blood relation, I fear you hold no claim to this unfortunate creature, and I must request that you step aside, sir," came her derisive and emasculating retort.

"She may be of no blood relation, but if she should survive — and may God grant it so — she will be welcomed into our home as if she were the daughter that might have been. And should she succumb to this tragedy, she will still remain under our care." Patty Cake was prone to a certain vein of docility, adopting the demeanour of the strong, silent type. These demonstrations were occasionally tested for theatrical effect, delivered not with menace or volume, but with the passionate insistence of his brusque plainness, emphasising that all should be treated as ordinary human beings. "In either case, Matron, she is now my responsibility. And in my view, no matter how you elevate yourself into your position in life so others marvel and you look down your nose to feel superior, it is the contents of your heart and the goodness of your actions that truly matter. If you feel compelled to speak, let your words be only those of kindness. I shall remain, you are now excused."

To this epitaph, Matron swallowed down her self-elevated pride and took her leave.

In an effort to console the grieving child, Sebelius's reassuring hand gently rested on her small shoulder and a surge of emotion devastated him, forcing him to recoil. The child, with unwavering intensity, radiated a fervent and shattering desire, in the form of her unyielding wish. Her wishes, hopes, and prayers were as intense as those of any living soul who gathered around the beds of their loved ones, hoping for their recovery and strength. However, this tiny child harboured a different desire. She did not yearn for her mother to awaken and receive care from the kind baker and his wife. No, what the child desired, with equal parts love and longing, was for her mother to succumb to her illness, to release herself, and in doing so, join her daughter in the realm of spirits where she was needed most. This child, wise beyond her years, understood that if her mother lived, she could not remain with her until fate's bidding brought death. There had to be closure, an end and finality, where the living must carry on and those who had passed must find rest. She wished for her mother's peace, knowing it meant they could be together, undisturbed by the boundaries of life and death.

"Whatever's the matter?" the burly baker asked his friend, who uttered not a single word in reply. Instead, he simply prompted Patty to hover his hand near the spirit of the grieving child, a gesture that conveyed all the little girl's hopes and prayers for a reunion with her mother. Laidey understood that she could never return to her mother in the living world, so the very being who gave her life now needed to sacrifice herself so they could be together in eternal rest.

"All will be well, Sebelius," his father assured him as he approached. Amidst the chaos, Patty took a seat beside the woman, and the spirits of Sebelius, his father, Lust, and Pride gathered around her bed.

"Father, I'm sorry. You did what you did to protect me, knowing I would get hurt regardless of the outcome. Pain was inevitable. But you gave me a pain that was lessened and bearable, easier to carry, than a greater one that would have always been present and would have pulled at my very soul," Sebelius reflected. "I am truly sorry."

"It is I who should apologise. I should have told you the truth, but I tried to spare you because you would have questioned every part of your being, as I did. I wished every day, for a long time after your mother left, that I were a greater prospect, a better prize, a champion of her heart, an exceptional man. But I could only be me, as you could only be you, and you have no room to be more kind-hearted, considerate, purer, or innocent, because you are all those things in infinite abundance. Neither of us was enough to make her stay, because we, neither of us, were him."

In his convivial inclination to entertain and infuse levity into the dire situation, Patty recounted his visit to Bayswater, causing him to burst into rapturous laughter at the reimagining of the event. As others looked on, they observed that he was not demented, but simply regaling the young lady who lay motionless out of her inert state. Even Sebelius joined in, cajoling the baker with jovial wordplay on the matter, which earned him his father's scornful, "Sebelius!" Oh, how he missed his name being spoken by him.

"I do think you and I are soon to be redundant," Lust acknowledged with a heavy acceptance to her companion. Pride nodded with a smile.

"You aren't going anywhere, Lady Milbrow," Sebelius interjected. "I will need you until the end of time, if that is agreeable to you?"

"Very," she replied with her face aglow, in that way only she could. She perched at the end of the bed and naturally placed her hand upon Laidey's arm, causing her face to drop with absolute horror.

"There is still much to be done, and now I must depart home for Christmas. Mrs Perkins will move my bed to the alleyway if this face, no matter how dishevelled it looks, does not make an appearance," Patty complained.

"Never you mind, sir, you be off," one of the passing nurses reassured him, mistakenly believing him to be addressing the patient. "We will take real good care of her until you come again."

The nurse approached her duties with a cheerful grin upon receiving Patty's heartfelt gratitude and, when out of earshot, bid the company farewell.

Sebelius followed, casting an unintentional glance toward the window where he paused. Patty turned his attention in the same direction and saw what caused Sebelius's clear rush of emotion — beyond the window hovered a tormented, pitiful spectre, pleading sorrowfully. It was evident that this repugnant apparition was known to his friend.

"What deplorable cacodemon is that?" Patty hissed.

"That is the creature who let me drown and took the charity funds as his reward!" Sebelius said scornfully. "What could he possibly want?"

It was indeed the man who left Sebelius to die, aimlessly floating and never knowing peace. Condemned to his slavery of shackles borne of every ill-gotten gain, endless misdeed, and ceaseless cruelty, the spectre hovered mid-air outside the window of the ward, observing the sick and needy, longing to help, but found himself powerless to act, his human form no longer tethered to the ability to intervene. His pleading eyes bore into one thing alone in that room, Sebelius himself. He turned his gaze away from the fiend and saw, for the first time, the young boy who had lain lifeless and alone when they had entered, now recognisable by the presence of his family, namely his father. He was the man who had snatched his child from Sebelius's icy grip. He shot a look towards the window again, the demon was gone.

The doors closed upon the ward, and Sebelius seized the moment to reveal to his friend the identity of the lifeless child. In response, Patty swiftly returned to the ward, intent on speaking with the grieving family without seeking any direction from his companion, so as not to risk encountering discouragement or disapproval.

"I fear, sir, that if you have come to gladden the hearts of the children upon this blessed day, then your task may be greater here than you anticipated," the distraught and dishevelled man said to Patty in reference to his attire. "He has not stirred since the accident," the boy's father continued, his eyes transfixed upon the unresponsive face. The child's mother sat at the bedside, with one of his hands cradled in both of hers.

"It's a miracle that he has survived thus far, and he is in the prayers of the nation, of that I am sure," Patty assured him, requesting a private moment with the grieving gentleman away from the ward, escaping the constant whir of activity and suffering. With hastened strides, they left the sterile confines behind and departed from the child's bedside into the corridor.

"Please be brief, sir. We only have today. Tomorrow, I shall be back at my desk. I should be there this day, but I am here on compassionate ground, so it is said, although he will stop me half-a-crown for it. He hasn't one shred of compassion in him," the man muttered insensibly. "Oh, you wouldn't look upon me this way if you knew Mr—" he paused, remembering himself in that paranoid fashion where one admonishes an employer, quite justifiably, but feels overly exposed for doing so, and thus supplied no conclusion to the sentence. He knew better than to chastise the name of the man who fed his family, even if it was a meagre pittance.

His face, gaunt and troubled, had clearly not seen a moment's rest since the incident, and his eyes were bloodshot and sore from the constant deluge of tears.

"Oh sir, I fear he will die," he responded when Patty asked about the child's progress. "I am so afraid, so dreadfully afraid!" His tone escalated into a frenzy of dismal excitement. "I'm so painfully afraid that he'll succumb, leaving me behind, and everyone blaming me for his demise! But I needn't fret, for if he perishes, surely I'll follow, my heart will shatter beyond repair. Of that I'm certain."

"Not at all, my good man," reassured the baker, accustomed to the lucid confessions of men, particularly when inebriated, and ordinarily as the result of fate's cruelty, and all its manifestations. "Not at all!"

"I swear it," he muttered, his right fist clenched as it pounded into the palm of his left. "I swear it, if he dies, they shall only have to dig the hole once, because they will bury me with him."

There were no offerings from Patty to the grieving man's ravings of grief; instead, he simply placed his large, burly hand upon the man's shoulder. Then, he posed his question, "I wanted to ask you about the man who saved your child, sir?"

"What man?" the father retorted amongst his sobs.

"A young man, his name, Sebelius Sallow, saved your child."

"No, sir. You are mistaken," he said with eyes darting in every direction, trying to recall the event that he fought so hard to suppress. "I saved my boy, sir. I pulled him from the water myself," he concluded assuredly, but Patty challenged him gently to think harder upon his recollection. He began again, "I am sure of it, but if what you tell me is correct, then show me this fellow and I will bestow a thousand thanks, for I am a poor man and my gratitude is all the comfort I might offer in way of a reward."

"Sebelius Sallow perished in the saving of your child."

The tormented father's eyes darted along every course as he tried to recall the tragic event and with this came the spluttering of denial and incredulity.

"Lor' knows you've enough to contend with, and I don't tell you this to add to your upset. It is only fair that a man, who surrendered his time here upon this earth so that your son could go forth in his life, should be acknowledged and mentioned," Patty said.

"How?" The shattered man paused and started again in his rambling manner, "How do you know this? Who told you of this fantastical tale? Were you present?"

"I have a certain gift, though my wife might call it a curse." Patty fell silent so he might begin anew. "The aforementioned gentleman befriended me this morning, and I speak only the truth because I do not wish to add to your grief."

"First you recount the tale of a man that died in the saving of my little child's life, yet you claim to have 'befriended' him this morning?" The father's countenance turned a darker shade. "Are you quite well, sir? I suspect, judging by your attire and your demented ramblings, you are fresh out of Bedlam and you wish to bring even more dis-jointed misery to what should be a joyous occasion. My son lies there on the brink of death and you bring me this nonsense?"

"Close your eyes, sir," Patty said as he took the man by the elbow stunting his retreat back to the sorrow of his child's sick bed. "If only to prove me wrong, close your eyes." The man yielded to the request, as Patty instructed, "Come, Sebelius, show the gentleman—"

Hearing his name, the gentleman's eyes sprang open, showing unease and prompting him to excuse himself back into the ward. Sebelius stepped forward and placed the flat of his hand upon the man's breast, fusing him to the spot where he stood, his inner self falling back, immersed and drowning in a sea of pure darkness and ice. Sebelius conveyed the tragedy of his whole experience.

The ordeal resonated deeply, causing the agonised man to burst into a fit of screaming tears, and, dropping to the bony, malnourished joints of his knees before Patty's skirts, he confessed. "I saw... I saw... saw it! Mark my words, I saw it all, that brave, brave man. Mark me down, the physical pain in which that man died in saving my little child, is the same pain I feel still, there is no other like it. If my son dies, ask those bearers of medicine... and Mr Sallow... to let me be and allow me to die!" he wailed and the flood of tears from both eyes and nose ran down the creases of his wretched face and into his mouth.

"Your child will live, and it's our duty that all shall know the name of the one who saved him," Patty said as he brought the man back to his feet. "You must wash yourself of your pain before you return to your wife. She will not wish to see weak eyes. Be strong." The man departed, to fortify himself before his re-entry into the ward.

Any thought of returning home to the welcoming embrace of his wife and the cheerful greetings of regular patrons at his beloved inn was abruptly postponed, as the reappearance of Alfredo Rossi-Esposito-Santoro-Tassoni dashed those hopes to the ground.

XVII

The persistent knocking on the front door, starting with a modest single rap and gradually escalating into a barrage of vigorous knocks fired in rapid succession, interrupted Bethell's task of cleaning the family plate at the table. His enjoyment of the harmonious carols drifting from the nearby church and the benefit of being seated meant he struggled to assemble the energy to address the disturbance and silently hoped the visitors would disappear.

The knocking grew more insistent, defying Bethell's desire to remain where he was. He began to relinquish the notion that it was merely carollers at the door, suspecting instead that someone with urgent business awaited entry.

"Mr Cake? Really—" Bethell began his protest as the visitor burst over the threshold.

"Mr Bravington, where is he?"

"He is not at home!"

With an ungracious clamour, Patty pushed further into the hallway. "Where is he, Bethell?" he barked, whirling suddenly as he called out for him in a booming voice, "Bravington! Bravington!"

"He isn't here, sir. I have told you. What is the meaning of this?"

"I was told he was troubled. I thought he might be here. Is he not back from the undertaker? We need to go in search of him!"

"Patty!" Sebelius called out as he stood on the pavement. "He's returned."

The baker hastened from the house and joined his friend on the pavement, the hairs alive upon his arms and neck to the rhythmic cadence of hooves upon the cobbles. It was the gradual swell of clip-clopping and the grumble of wheels upon the solid stones that caused a flow of anticipation to course through Patty's veins. He pressed his back against the sturdy black railings that stood sentinel, just in time to witness a scene of unexpected elegance unfolding before his eyes.

A hansom carriage glided forth serenely, its sleek form gracefully navigating a circular lap around the church. Behind it followed a procession of three funeral carriages, each a vision of sombre opulence. The first two were identical hearses, drawn by a pair of muscular tenebrous horses adorned with black plumes, harnesses, and intricate gold embellishments. Within the carriages of gleaming etched glass rested coffins of the most luxurious wood, the brass accents shining brightly in the sunlight.

In the second hearse, a discernible difference was apparent — a smaller vessel, crafted from the same rich wood, cradled the precious remains of a child. The third carriage bore Mr Cannadine and his men, who sat dignified in their duty. Such a sight was this marvel to behold, it caused the passersby to pause in reverence. Gentlemen respectfully removed their hats, while gentlewomen bowed their heads in solemn acknowledgment. The hansom carriage swept gracefully before Patty, then halted a few houses further, making way for the convoy.

Aubrey Bravington alighted the carriage, his inflamed eyes fell upon a familiar face, one he was so very glad to see — Patty Cake.

"I'm in there," Sebelius Sallow said to the baker, as they both stood staring, Patty's reflection mirrored in the glass. There was a half-expectation on his part to see Sebelius's reflection next to him, momentarily forgetting that the being, who had caused so much upheaval to his Christmas and elicited such profound emotions in the giant man, was no longer of the living world.

"Bethell, prepare the house for our Christmas guests," Bravington instructed his faithful manservant.

"Is it wrong to say that this is a spectacle of great beauty?" Patty observed to the flame-headed man.

"I am honoured that you should think so. They had placed him in pine. I couldn't allow it. After all he has done and for all he means, I couldn't allow it."

"It's more than fitting."

"Where is he?" Bravington inquired. He searched for Sebelius, harbouring an unspoken fear that he might depart as suddenly as he had earlier that day. Yet, at the centre of this worry, a flicker of hope burned within him — that he had done enough to earn absolution so that the friend he once knew might reveal himself once more.

"He is just there," Patty said, extending a quiet arm in the direction of the extraction point where the coffin was to be lifted from the carriage. Once more, Patty's heart broke looking at the solitary figure. Sebelius stood, gazing at his coffin, and, without a sound, Mr Cannadine and his four men bowed at the hearses and proceeded to remove the adult coffin first. Sebelius said nothing and watched intently as they approached with respect, observing the four men carrying him upon their shoulders and following their master, while Bravington walked behind in his duty as chief mourner.

Closing his eyes, Sebelius whispered, "Lady Milbrow, please come. Father, I need you. Laidey, come and see." Immediately upon the last word, the subjects of his request stood next to him. "Closure comes, Father," he said, pressing his cheek against his father's face. Sebelius lowered himself to meet the child. "We are to be together, Laidey," he told her as he embraced her in a hug.

"What about Mother?"

"There have been considerations made for her, so whenever she joins us, she will have a place with us on earth and especially here with us in spirit," he reassured her. "Mr Bravington has sorted everything."

"Am I in there?" she asked inquisitively, tilting her head in childlike astonishment.

"Yes, and you're all warm and safe, and more importantly, you are at peace with me, and Pa, and, one day, your mother too."

"And Mr Aubrey and Mr Cake?"

"One day, when it's their time, and not before. We all have our time."

The gentlemen of Cannadine and Smidge emerged, and in the same mechanical act, they took the smaller coffin. Following Mr Cannadine, the men advanced, Patty followed, and then Sebelius, Laidey, Enoch, and Lady Milbrow.

Soon, the dutiful subjects of Mr Cannadine, and indeed the man himself, took their leave to the clamour of hooves that ricocheted around the square, a pageantry that once again filled the witnesses' eyes with wonder. The windows of the room where Sebelius and Laidey lay were shuttered, a merry fire danced on the hearth, casting a warm glow throughout the room. The lamps burned brightly, illuminating familiar corners with a welcoming light. The clock greeted the room with its old, familiar tick-tock and bing-bong, a comforting sound that brought life to the quiet space. Everything was serene, warm, and inviting — a stark contrast to the manufactured ambience of hope and comfort Bravington had left behind at Mr Cannadine's.

"You have done a tremendous thing, Mr Bravington," Patty said joyfully. "A truly tremendous thing."

"Thank goodness for these," Bravington affirmed, withdrawing the blue documents from his inside pocket, bearing Sebelius's handwritten final wishes that his hand had facilitated. "You do understand that I couldn't leave him there, alone, at Christmas, or the child?" Bravington's deviation from the original plan was prompted by seeing his dear friend laid out in an unfitting coffin and unfamiliar surroundings. "In life, it was only the familiar that had truly brought him comfort, so I really couldn't leave him there."

Seven bodies remained unclaimed, and it was agreed that if they remained so by the twenty-ninth day of that holy month, their burial costs would be sent to Aubrey Bravington at Smith's Square, and they would be buried on the thirty-first day alongside the two now resting beneath his roof.

"New Year's Eve?" Patty acknowledged thoughtfully. "Yes, let them rest as they see the old year out and the new year in. On that note, it's just past three o'clock, and I should be making a move towards home. Will you be alright, Mr Bravington?"

The subject of Patty's concern standing with his face down, eyes closed, and a gentle hand resting on the wooden lid of his friend's coffin, replied, "I shall be more than alright." As he watched the coarse man, whom he had grown fond of in such a short space of time, turn to leave, he bid, "Merry Christmas, Patty."

"Merry Christmas, Aubrey," Patty replied. He gave a genuine smile, reserved for those to whom it was truly meant, before departing.

Having poured himself a large brandy and standing before the hearth, twirling the amber contents before the flames, Bravington's gaze periodically drifted between the imposing, smooth, dark polished case, where, he reminded himself, his beloved friend lay.

"If you are content for these eyes to look upon you, Sebelius Sallow, then they will be glad to see you," he said, taking a hearty sip from the glass, and he looked around expectantly.

In an act of propriety, Lady Milbrow deemed it appropriate for Sebelius's companions to depart. Laidey vanished to the place she most desired to be, while Enoch and the lustful spirit followed along after her.

The artist's soft, silky hands glided along the glossy, varnish-smooth surface of Sebelius's casket. His fingers were warmed by the rich hue of the wood, basking in the glow of the flames. Speaking as freely aloud to Sebelius as he had when they sat together in Mr Cannadine's establishment, he removed the lid to reveal his friend in statuesque peace. Placing the lid upright against the wall, Bravington's eyes traced Sebelius's name on the brass plaque that bore the years of his entry and departure from this world, a world he was always destined to be too good for.

Bravington's reflection shimmered in the brass, his fiery hair and weary eyes rendering him, in his own estimation, a dishevelled mess.

"I think you look quite beautiful," Sebelius's voice whispered like the flame of a flickering candle, drawing his friend's gaze back to the plaque, but only etched letters and his own reflection could be seen. Startled, he turned sharply, only to find Sebelius wasn't there. Whirling back to the brass, Bravington paused, and took a breath, he was greeted by Sebelius's reflection, which showed him to be set further back in the room. He turned briskly once more, but Sebelius was nowhere in sight.

"Forget these tricks, Sebelius Sallow. If you can reveal yourself to a humble baker, then you can do so to a lowly artist," he chided gently.

Peering once more at the plaque, he beheld Sebelius, standing vigilantly beside his outstretched, peaceful form, with his hands resting on the edge of the chosen casket. Turning again, Bravington's friend remained, no longer concealed, prompting him to take his place on the opposing side of the spirit, fashioning his hands upon the edge. "I will forever be grateful for what you did," Sebelius expressed sincerely.

"I blame myself," Bravington conceded.

"You had no hand in this," Sebelius absolved him.

"I came to the shop but I was delayed."

"I know that now," Sebelius confirmed with a greater understanding. "You were cajoled into painting-in the newly acquired medals awarded to Colonel Cecil-Yule on the portrait that hangs in his home. I've seen it, it's a perfect likeness."

"He's a horrid, bullish man. I should have told him to wait."

"No one says no to Colonel Cecil-Yule," Sebelius scoffed. "Not even my mother, she married him. Wasn't dead at all, but left Father and me. That was the tale to spare my feelings."

Bravington's mind snagged at the news, having had some inkling of this phenomenon, and the explanation could only be attributed to the intertwining of their existences during the seance.

Much of their shared experiences had likely been buried within the recesses of subconscious thought.

"I have so much to say," Bravington sighed, his voice heavy and his mind filled with unspoken words.

"Then speak it." Sebelius seemed to gleam with a certain anticipation.

"I am at a loss now." Bravington wasn't sure if his mind was a blank canvas or a crude mess of dense emotions and misspent actions, built up in thick layers. Each form of suppression had varnished them solidly, leaving no opportunity for removal.

"Well, it's all very well that I know it already."

"I am so sorry I was delayed, and for abandoning you when we parted ways at school. I'm sorry for all of it."

"I know all about that too," Sebelius confirmed.

Finding himself penitently offering apologies time and again, Bravington's repetition of regret carried the weight of true remorse. It seemed as though no matter how many times he expressed his contrition, it could never fully erase the guilt that burdened his conscience.

"You have no reason to be sorry."

"I want to be," insisted Bravington, with a gaze that pleaded forgiveness.

"Then prey continue." Sebelius smiled. "I know all you said when you sat with me at the undertakers. Spirits can be everywhere, you know."

"I regret nothing. All that I said, I shall never retract," Bravington insisted.

"Nor would I want you to, and I feel the same." The spirit, in a futile attempt to offer comfort, extended a tentative hand but quickly withdrew, retreating to the edge of the wooden box. Any solace that physical touch could provide had been exhausted earlier that day, and nothing could emulate that now.

"I wish you could just re-enter your body, like you did mine and come back to us," the artist blurted foolishly, and hopefully.

With a gentle smile, Sebelius shook his head. "I cannot, that body no longer works. When your time is up, it is up. You need more than a willing soul."

"But you returned to live again through me?" he persisted.

"I shouldn't have, but no real harm was done. However, you know all there is to know of me," Sebelius replied.

"And do you now know all of me?" Bravington asked, suddenly feeling his diffidence return, evident not only in the tone of his voice but in the flushing of his cheeks. This was not his usual demeanour, but one he often adopted in interactions with his old school friend.

Sebelius nodded sagely. "Though it's surprising what you can learn in the world of spirits," he teased gently.

"I came by the shop intentionally. You cannot imagine my excitement when Earl Grey said he had a watch in need of repair. I'd wanted to come for weeks, months—"

"Surely, you mean years?" his friend taunted.

Embarrassment flushed Bravington's cheeks with an intensity that almost mirrored the flaming crown that adorned his head and the beard that neatly decorated his exquisite features. "And there you were," he concluded with gladness.

"What did you hope would happen?" Sebelius asked.

"Not this," he exclaimed with passion. "I hoped for time... where I could make amends, that included more of you... more of us. A time when you might sit awkwardly once more in a chair while I unknowingly sketched you. A time that would see us travel foreign lands so we could escape the confines of this gilded cage. We would have been free to travel as friends, best friends even. I hoped to paint you, and read to you. To try and sponge away the sadness that others had inflicted on you during those years before, during, and after having met you. If we only had time. I could speak to you in sentences that spoke of love, and now time is lost." There was a long pause as his confessions unearthed deeper layers within him. "I'm sorry I was too late," Bravington's broken voice uttered under the weight of his guilt.

"You arrived when it mattered," Sebelius said with a smile. "I'm sorry I had to leave you."

"You haven't left, you've just gone on ahead."

The clamorous day of Christmas gently yielded to what all hoped would be a silent night; the fading sun bestowed its final golden touch upon the cross crowning the zenith of St. Paul's. Twilight entered with the tribute of a gentle smattering of snow, and Sebelius Sallow remained in the company of his friend until he closed his eyes and was called to sleep.

But, just before this, Sebelius had a confession for his friend. "I think there is something you should know." This stirred curiosity in Bravington's mind. "Do you remember telling me that you believed that the morning chorus signalled to the other birds of them having survived the night?"

"Yes," Bravington replied, mystified.

"It's absolutely true," Sebelius replied, to which they both laughed. Aubrey drifted comfortably asleep, the laughter echoing in his mind, he never saw his friend again. Only when he closed his eyes for the final time many years later did he, upon opening them again, see the face of his dear old friend — the only person who ever truly held his heart — greeting him.

Epilogue

So, that is how Sebelius Sallow came to be.

Came to be what?

That is a very good question. If I do not tell you, then I wouldn't be much good, would I?

I began this story having accused you of not knowing Sebelius Sallow, nor having ever seen him. Now you do know him, and have seen him. Yes, even before you gave me your full attention in the telling of his story.

I shall continue from where we left off, and move quickly on from there, as there are still a few loose threads.

Early on Boxing Day morning, Aubrey Bravington awoke upon the floor in front of the spent embers of the fire. He recalled placing the fattest of logs upon the flames a few hours before, urging himself to combat his lethargy and fatigue. However, it was the comfort of his friend's company and the warmth of the flame that lulled him to sleep. Now, he had only the lifeless effigy of his friend to converse with, and he did so, every moment he could until New Year's Eve. However, the conversation went in only one direction.

Around the same time, Laidey woke on the empty bed where her mother lay unresponsive. In a frantic state of spiritual despair, the child called and wailed for her mother. Her cries were so pained, that Sebelius, his father, and his faithful Lady Milbrow did all within their power to console her. There was no sign of her mother until a bereft and inconsolable Laidey felt the customary touch of a hand within hers. It could only be that of her mother, who shone before her in an angelic form, without blemish or trace of her demise.

"I didn't think I should ever see you again," Laidey said in her lispy tone, which her mother had missed so very much.

"What have I told you, Diligence is a virtue, Laidey, and the desires of the diligent will be fully satisfied," her mother said, embracing her tightly into her bosom.

"I have met her, mother. She is very beautiful," Laidey told her gleefully, then introduced her friends one by one, to which the grateful mother showered her daughter's protectors with heartfelt thanks.

"Are you the spirit of Diligence, Laidey tells me of?" her mother asked Lust presumptively.

"Me? Absolutely not," the seductress protested in surprise, tailoring her response respectfully. "She is very charming and all, as Laidey says, but I'm far too outrageous. No, I'm—"

"Lady Milbrow," Sebelius barged in, supplying the conclusion of the introduction.

"That is I," Lust concluded melodically in joyful agreement, to which Laidey's mother conveyed her charm of their introduction. The reinvented lady rested a devoted glance at Sebelius, and concluded, "I am Lady Milbrow."

Having fully embraced his spiritual self, Sebelius found solace in the ethos of acceptance. No longer did he pine for his restoration to flesh and blood, longing to walk once more as a living iteration of unfinished love, and so began the final stage — that of genuine acceptance.

"Bonjour, Monsieur Sallow," said a voice well known to Lady Milbrow.

"It is as if they do not get enough joy up there," Lady Milbrow encouraged, looking up with a grimace as the final incarnation of the deadly sins appeared before them, and she was extremely deadly.

"I don't understand—" Sebelius said, confused.

"Sebelius Sallow, please allow me to introduce you to the spiritual incarnation of Gluttony, or the Comtesse Deauville." She gave her introduction through sumptuous lips that curled as she spoke her name, as the subject of her feelings gently moulded her powdered coiffure, enriched with pearls at the centre of the intricate curls and feathers.

"The Comtesse Deauville, the same person who—" Sebelius spoke but was stunted.

"The very same," Lady Milbrow said with an agitation that showed in the disquiet of her fingers.

"You are looking remarkably well, Mademoiselle Milbrow, at least since the last time I saw you!" The Comtesse's voice sang with the cadence of her French accent. "I see that you managed to get the gravel out of your face?"

"Indeed, when I regained spiritual consciousness, I plucked the pieces out one by one and turned them into pearls and beaded this very gown."

"You haven't seen one another since the accident?" Sebelius asked.

"It wasn't an accident, she pushed me out of a window!" Lady

Milbrow exclaimed. "And no, I quite rightly became the embodiment of Lust because I turn heads, and she became Gluttony, because, despite her tiny frame, she can put the food away at an alarming rate, and therefore she turns stomachs."

"I am excited to meet you, Monsieur Sallow. We will make a fabulous acceptance together. I know it."

"She appears to be quite lovely," Sebelius observed.

"Don't be fooled by that perfectly painted porcelain phizog, Sebelius Sallow! Did I mention she pushed me through a window?"

"What do you want me to do?" The horologist pleaded for a solution.

"Send her away," she commanded.

"I can't do that," he protested.

"You can!" Gripping his lapel she said, "And you must. Go on."

"Can you not do it?"

"Absolutely not."

"Why?"

"She is not here for me. Now, let's be done with her." This was followed by a hard stare, laden with the threat of impending death; though ultimately futile, it had not lost any semblance of menace.

"A thousand apologies, Comtesse—" he began.

"Do hurry up," Lady Milbrow admonished vivaciously, which came with the rolling of eyes.

"Comtesse, forgive me, I—" he began again.

"Hélène, would you please do us all the honour, which will earn you my eternal gratitude," Lady Milbrow whispered over her shoulder to her nemesis, "of throwing yourself from that window over there?"

The aristocrat, with lips parted to protest, ceased in her cause when her nemesis intervened again. "You may leave of your own accord, or I can help you through it, but rest assured, I do not need to wait until your back is turned."

"Is this your wish?" Gluttony turned to her charge, and he nodded ashamedly in agreement.

The Parisian gracefully retraced her steps from the gathering, and with each backward movement of her embroidered skirts, the window of the ward gradually lifted until, upon her arrival, it stood wide open. Sebelius approached, seemingly poised to offer an apology for the less-than-warm reception, but, raising her hand, she signalled him to halt. He complied. Conveying a few kind words in her native tongue, which Sebelius took to interpret as, "Do not boast about tomorrow, for you do not know what a day may bring," a smile graced her lips before she gracefully receded, merging into the enveloping darkness of morning that stirred, joining the celestial company fulfilling their Christmas obligations in the sky.

"I should have helped her along the way." Lady Milbrow motioned a shove of her hands as she spoke.

"That's not kind," Sebelius lambasted his friend.

"Me, unkind? Do you know what she just said to me? 'Do not boast about tomorrow, for you do not know what a day may bring,'" the temptress quoted. "Those were the very words Sloth said to me when I first arrived here in spirit," she informed them in answer to their puzzled looks.

"Did my daughter not have the support of these vices and virtues you mention?" Laidey's mother asked.

"No, she did not," Lady Milbrow responded firmly, to which the mother appeared a little aggrieved. "She had far better, for she was placed in the safekeeping of Sebelius and Enoch Sallow. They kept her safe and tended to her heartbroken cries, and they upheld their promise that they would reunite her with her mother. No one could have wished better for their child."

London was still heartily preoccupied by the mournful event of Christmas Eve; the haunting cries of newspaper sellers resounded louder than ever before, with Christmas having subdued the vigour of their usual voice into a respectful silence, marking the festive occasion. From every street corner they bellowed, serving to bring forth a loved one or an acquaintance of those missing. Crowds of morbidly curious onlookers descended en masse upon the scene where the tragic events had unfolded on that chilling Christmas Eve. Queen Victoria herself graced the site with her presence, witnessing a scene far more grave than when she passed by on that fateful late-afternoon.

The investment bore fruit. With each resounding call from the stands peddling their paper and print, and the poignant interviews with onlookers and survivors, much-needed attention was drawn to those who had perished. Among those telling their story was the father of the child saved by the heroic deed of Sebelius Sallow, marking the only time his name appeared in black and white. By the end, only three of the deceased remained unaccounted for — suspected wanderers of no fixed abode or solitary revellers who ventured onto the ice in isolated merriment, their absence unnoticed by any other living soul. True to his word, Aubrey Bravington ensured they would not be forgotten. On the same afternoon of her passing, Laidey's mother was retrieved and laid out by Cannadine and Smidge, thanks to the intervention of the Covent Garden baker and publican.

On New Year's Eve, precisely one week since the tragedy unfolded, the funeral procession meandered slowly through the streets and thoroughfares, departing from the funeral home promptly at one o'clock. Two black four-wheeler carriages and their customary black horses, carrying the funeral directors and their men, led the gloomy journey. They advanced in tandem, sandwiching six glass hearse carriages. The first two were adorned only with magnificent bursts of lilies in the absence of the coffins belonging to Sebelius Sallow and Laidey Brindle. The remaining four were occupied by the mortal remains of Laidey's mother, Mary Brindle, and the three unidentified victims.

"Where are they, Bethell? They should have arrived long before now!" Bravington exclaimed, his handsome features shrouded in the deepest black attire, to reflect what he himself thought to be the mourning of his forever broken heart.

"I am certain, sir, Messrs Cannadine and Smidge have everything under control—" his butler reassured him, just as a thud at the front door reverberated through every wall. Bravington, feeling a burst of relief, stuttered reassurances to his faithful servant. With gentle hands steadying the butler's shoulders, he positioned the old man and hurried to answer the door himself.

"Who in Heaven's name are you?" Bravington remonstrated with the two well-presented visitors standing before his open door. He, a burly, thick-set man with a kind face adorned with stubble and side whiskers, was attired in impeccable gentleman's attire, tailored to perfection. Beside him stood his dutiful wife, elegantly clad in garments of sorrow, specifically purchased for the occasion.

"Do you not recognise your new friend, Mr Bravington?" the gentleman retorted in a deep, familiar voice, prompting the artist to scrutinise him more closely.

"Patty Cake!" Bravington exclaimed, seizing his hand and shaking it heartily with a blend of trepidation, nervousness, and surprise. Due to the baker's business commitments and the artist's responsibility in arranging the final farewell to his friend, they had conversed daily through written word but never in person. "I didn't recognise you, my friend. And you must be—" the artist began, only to be interrupted by the subject of surprise, who took the liberty of introducing herself as Mrs Perkins, the expectation of being called 'Cake' having long lost its appeal.

"Calm down, there will be a perfectly good explanation. Give them another thirty minutes, and if they aren't here, we will send a boy along," Patty reassured him, and indeed, a perfectly good reason was the cause.

What was anticipated as a quiet, private procession evolved into a pageantry beyond all expectations. The streets overflowed with mourners, eager to pay their final respects. Among them were witnesses, survivors, those who had lost loved ones, and those who had heard or read of the tragedy, for scarcely a soul remained untouched by the devastating events. As the carriages passed, spectators joined in, walking behind in silence, punctuated only by the creaking of wheels, the gentle cadence of clopping hooves, the tap of shoe leather on cobbled roads, and the muffled swish of skirts.

The mood had long since buckled under the onerous oppression of stillness. Lady Milbrow's delicate voice imploded the silence, sending invisible shards of noiseless grief to fall around them. Her melodious tones carried the sacred notes of 'Silent Night'. Sebelius stood transfixed, surrendered to the haunting poignancy of the tune that had once comforted him in the face of the inevitable separation of body and soul. It drifted through the frigid stillness, this token of past comfort performed to soothe present sorrow. With a gesture of her hand, Lady Milbrow beckoned the mourners to join in, their participation involuntary yet deeply resonant in a chorus of reverent sorrow. In these moments, our differences fade, for we are all equal in grief. When we shed tears at one funeral, we aren't solely grieving for that individual; we are essentially mourning the loss of all those who have departed our lives before them.

Arriving at the square, the sentiment of quaking shepherds, hosts singing alleluias and love's pure light transcended words, settled into a respectful melodic hum. The commotion stirred Bethell, who awaited at the window, drawing the residents of the sleepy square out onto the pavement. They were met with an impressive sight.

Sebelius and Laidey were the first to emerge from the house, guided carefully across the cobbled square and up the stone steps into the quaint church nestled at its heart. Then, with the same adoration, the remaining vessels were carried in. Among the sparse number of invitees, representing Sebelius were Bravington, Patty Cake, his wife, and the hero's mother, Effie Cecil-Yule. She came alone, having not seen her husband since her belongings were packed and she vacated Bayswater on Boxing Day, never to return. No one came for Mary Brindle and her little child, whom no one had thought of since she was abandoned by her mistress due to her husband's impropriety which ultimately led to motherhood. However, they, along with the three unidentified individuals — two females and a male — would be represented by the countless thousands who filled the outside space and surrounded the church.

The service commenced with a choir of seventy voices, yet, as Bravington surveyed the emptiness of the splendid space and perceived the injustice of the vacant pews, he swung wide the doors, extending a heartfelt welcome to all until every inch of standing room had been claimed. Among the first faces he encountered, waiting upon the top step, were the father and mother of the young boy whom Sebelius had sacrificed himself to save. They stood with their four small children, with the noticeable absence of one — the child Sebelius had rescued. Bravington's spirits were lifted to hear that the boy had not perished but was instead recuperating in the hospital, grappling with the aftermath of the accident's lasting complications, which would forever be substantial. Bravington welcomed them to sit with him, for he too was alone in the world now that his engagement to Lady Georgiana had ceased with the classic, "The fault lies not with you, but with myself," and that she should "go and marry a greater man than I." But Georgiana Grey never would, and never did.

All the spirits of the tragedy gathered, unseen but deeply felt, and the service gave way to ceremony while Bravington's eyes gave way to bitter tears and his handkerchief comforted his fierce sobs. What should have unfolded with swifter precision instead lingered, drawing the proceedings to a close past three o'clock. Before the six vessels departed the sacred sanctuary, final blessings were spoken aloud, intermingling with whispered wishes and the emergence of new hope. The choir hummed the haunting tune engraved in the memory of the timepiece crafted by Sebelius's hand — 'London Waits'; indeed, London was prepared to wait. The hum of voices resonated through the space with the intensity of grief, and the coffins were lifted into their carriages, embarking on their journey to the Cemetery of All Souls in the Royal Borough of Kensington and Chelsea. The echo of the choir's bittersweet lament continued along the route to quell the sound of emptiness.

The four miles of road continued to be lined, and a procession on foot still followed behind until clusters were lost, bit by bit, to the public houses that stood on corners or hid up back alleys, until only the faithful remained. Not one section of road remained unlit, and, as dusk fell, the final prayers were being said.

"By the sweat of your brow you will eat your food until you return to the ground, since from it you were taken; for dust you are and to dust you will return."

Sebelius, Laidey, her mother, and the three unknown spirits, who Sebelius and his spiritual companions came to know intimately, took one another's hands and subsequently took their leave, as their mortal remains were now undisturbed, save for the thudding clamour of earth from the gravedigger's shovels that landed upon the lid of their coffins.

"Welcome, Sebelius Sallow, never was there a truer representation of your name," boomed the voice of Seraphim, the Chief Celestial Protector.

"My name?" Sebelius queried.

"Not that assigned to you at birth, but the one that is to be entrusted to you in death," the Protector proclaimed solemnly. "You are to be anointed as the spirit of 'Do As You Would Be Done By'."

Within the hallowed walls of St. Paul's Cathedral, the decree of consecration was reverently read — a choice made by Sebelius himself. Encircled by the Guardians who oversee the transition of souls, he was enveloped in a radiant light. They bestowed upon him the privilege to surpass the constraints of time, enabling him to seamlessly navigate between the physical and spectral realms. Entrusted with a sacred duty and honour, he was charged with upholding the guiding principles of justice, fairness, compassion, integrity, and generosity.

"Each of us possesses the glorious gift of choice. We have the power to determine what actions we find acceptable and how we wish to be treated. It is these intentions and actions that shape our experiences, both in the present and in the future, extending even beyond death. Positive actions inevitably yield positive outcomes, often not immediately apparent, while negative actions lead to regrettable consequences, affecting not only our spiritual essence but our mortal existence," Seraphim instructed.

And so he was, and so he is, even to this day, and shall persist until the very end of time, until every soul is spent, each one finding its rightful place in both body and spirit.

There are portraits that exist today of the great man, Sebelius Sallow. No, I did not lie to you when we set out upon this journey, I said there are no known portraits of him, but Aubrey Bravington did go on to be a marvellous portraitist. His name is seldom mentioned today, but occasionally his works might come up at an auction. This happens mainly when the lifeblood of a family line ceases, so contents are sold with no hands to gift the treasures of their existence. The artist continued to paint Sebelius from memory, using his studied sketches from when they were both at school, he painted him again and again. He immortalised him delicately as he might have aged, yet even then the effects of age had not changed him remarkably. Today, over a fireplace, in a house in Smith's Square, the former residence of Aubrey Bravington, there hangs a picture of a beautiful man, his hair the golden colour of buttered toast, his skin pale and flawless, his nose long, straight and proud, lips that have never uttered a curse against a living soul, and a chin in the shape of a delicate heart, and that man is Sebelius Sallow. Though I suspect no one knows it.

"I'll leave you with this," Patty said, his voice soft against the crackle of the fire, as he handed Bravington a long pale blue envelope, which he took with one hand as the other cradled a hefty brandy. The baker and his wife were about to take their leave from the room where Sebelius had rested in peaceful repose leading up to the funeral.

"Is he still here?" Bravington asked after a gulp of the fiery liquid, causing the baker and his wife to pause at the doorway.

Pained to answer, Patty shook his head. "No, I'm afraid not. He's needed elsewhere."

"But I was told he'd be here if I needed him, even if I couldn't see him."

"And so he will, but he's moving forward in the afterlife, and you must move forward in this one. Read his letter," Patty gently urged as they closed the door and departed.

As the letter slid from its envelope, Bravington sank to the floor before the gentle glow of the fire. Its contents will forever remain private, but what can be shared are Sebelius's final words upon the page:

With a hand that extends love, there inevitably emerges upon it, over time, the shadow of pain, unmarked but deeply felt. Love, though magnificent, carries within it a profound pain, piercing deeper than any physical blade forged by humanity.

Love, often perceived as intangible, manifests itself to be very real in the gentle touch of a hand, in eyes brimming with tears at mere thoughts, in the elation of hearing a cherished voice, and in the scent and flavour of affection, that saturates every experience embraced by love's essence.

Remember, too much grieving disturbs the dead. Keep not the grief alive, but the love.

I have not left you, I've simply gone on ahead.

Forever yours,
   Sebelius

Clutching the letter tightly, Bravington scolded himself for not following his heart and instead swayed by the opinions of others, adhering always to societal expectations. As the clock chimed midnight, heralding the arrival of the new year, he shut his eyes against the jubilant cheers rising from the square and the revelry of those around him. His ultimate regret weighed heavily: banishing his friend from his chamber on that cold Christmas Eve, leaving the vulnerable soul without the support of the one person he should have always been able to rely on.

It was this very action that caused Sebelius to act as drastically as he did — well, we will get to that in just a moment — yet, amidst his remorse, Bravington expressed gratitude for the steadfast loyalty of the humble baker who never abandoned him, and for that he was eternally grateful.

What do you think Sebelius did when he burst through the window after being shunned by his friend on that Christmas Eve night? You surely recall the event? The humiliation of his shattered spirit sent him spiralling into the lowest intensity of destruction, clinging to the hope that it might eventually lead to his salvation. He wished himself back, to return to his little shop, to the point where his living-self waited for his friend to arrive. His yearning stretched into an eternity of waiting, where the cold chains of reality began to tighten their grip around his heart, he conceded to the truth. Aubrey Bravington was not coming.

Sebelius's mortal hand delved into the depths of his coat pocket, and, withdrawing the key to the front door, he found within the crease of his fingers, a solitary sovereign nestled within.

"Buy something wonderful, or keep it, which I suspect you will. May it bring you luck if nothing else, dear sweet Sebelius." The spirit of Sebelius repeated Bravington's words aloud.

His mortal-self, who could hear them, responded, "You suspect, do you? Much like your anticipation that I would stand here waiting for you, which I am, taking you at your word?"

He placed the gifted sovereign into the regal blue pouch alongside the donations intended for the workhouse. Carefully, he pulled the gold drawstrings, securing the pouch, and tying a decisive knot, he looped the thread through his trousers, ensuring its safekeeping. His heart lightened with the generosity of the season, causing his bright eyes to gleam with a coruscating brown.

His broken spirit stood and stared deep into those pools, placing his hand upon the chest of his former self, which ceased him and ultimately caused an arsenal of icy spears to surge forth, piercing forward before recoiling in their outward retaliation, ushering in the discomfort of a heavy slump. Though his living embodiment could not see him, he experienced the deathly coldness upon his heart, and with it raged an onslaught of feelings, emotions and questions that were foreign to him.

For the time Sebelius stood with his arm outstretched, his former self stood still, his gaze wide with astonishment, glistening with tears. And, for as long as he stood there, he remained motionless.

"Sebelius! You must let him be," his father's voice pleaded from behind.

"If I can spare him, then I gladly will!" Sebelius exploded with a passion he could never muster to speak out loud when he had occupied the flesh. What if he had been bolder, harder, more like other people? Then he might still be alive. Wouldn't he? If he had a voice strong enough to stand up to everyone, and the courage to be with Aubrey Bravington without caring at all, would things have been different?

"The decision has been made. You cannot change it. But you are just delaying the inevitable. Look about you!" Enoch Sallow called.

Every clock had ceased in their useful purpose, paused of their ticking, silenced of tocking; the pendulums stood frozen. Yet his mortal self still lived and breathed, entranced by the sheer sensation of that which lay upon his heart. Reluctantly yielding to fate and all its inevitabilities, he removed his hand and the clocks regained their momentum. His living embodiment shook off his suspension, and, pacing forward to leave, he walked through the spirits of himself and his father as he departed for what lay ahead.

Sebelius Sallow, the incarnation of the spiritual essence we now revere, never revisited the past to observe his mortal self; he had truly transcended, embracing his fate and the imperative role of Do As You Would Be Done By.

The law of the spiritual realm dictates that our loved ones will always answer our call, even if it's by way of our fleeting thought.

Each day, Aubrey Bravington summoned Sebelius in mind, though unable to see him, his presence was always felt.

What happened to the clock?

My, you are nosey. It was gifted to Aubrey Bravington upon the passing of Sebelius's mother, who had reverted to the name of Sallow. The name gained much renown following the news of her son's heroics and tragic demise, known far and wide until her own passing, along with those who shared her era. They, of course, passed on the tale to their offspring, but as time tends to do, memories fade... until they're forgotten.

The clock remained in Smith's Square until the fiery-haired man's passing. Today, it hangs above a Sicilian marble mantelpiece in a grand New York mansion, nestled in the heart of Manhattan.

It's believed, and I ardently affirm its truth, that upon Bravington's final exhalation, Sebelius waited beside his friend, guiding him onwards. Seraphim's decree ordained the artist to ascend and become the spirit of Harmony in Every Action and Reaction, yet this proclamation remains uncertain, unlike that of Sebelius Sallow's own destiny. Perhaps you know better?

I often see Sebelius Sallow at the foot of my stairs, while I'm in the kitchen. Though he has appeared in other places, it's predominantly there. I ponder whether his presence is to acknowledge my recent deeds and actions, or if he extends across from one neighbour's side to the other. I assure you, you've glimpsed him too — it's that flicker in your peripheral vision, that fleeting shadow that momentarily puzzles the mind and makes you question your senses. He vanishes so swiftly that one cannot discern his form.

But mark this, Sebelius Sallow is everywhere, he watches, he knows, ensuring that no one is overlooked, for every intention carries its own repercussions — whether that intent comes from a place of good, or from that other extremity.

About The Author

Richie Joyce writes so that he may forget, and in order for him to always remember. The art of storytelling brings relief and purpose in facing the challenges of dyslexia and chronic nerve pain in his head and neck, stemming from a bout of shingles. Inspired by his two childhood passions of Christmas and the Victorian era (yes, it is true that he had a childhood crush on Prince Albert, and has never truly grown out of it), he remains devoted to both. The first by way of embodying the ethos; that it's not the Christmas things you do at Christmastime that count, but the Christmas things you do all year through. The second by dedicating himself to restoring his Victorian home, which he shares with a long suffering partner and an array of Victoriana (which said partner would gladly throw in the bin).

Acknowledgements

The problem with acknowledgments is that not everyone who matters can truly be acknowledged, and as someone with plenty to say, I must keep this succinct. Just know that you all matter.

Paul Swallow, my Editor extraordinaire, I owe you a debt of gratitude that words cannot fully express. The pride I feel knowing that someone as brilliantly talented as you wanted to shape and tailor my words is immeasurable — they are now a perfect fit. You may try to hide in the shadows, but we see you, we adore you, and we simply couldn't be ourselves without you.

My sister, **Caz Dirks** — I don't know where to begin. You are tremendous, a vibrant soul and one of life's most colourful characters. You believe in me even when I don't. We're on our way to those matching powder-blue Bentleys, my friend!

Angharad and **Thomas Bridge** — the family we choose and we love you. Your wedding will go down in history as being the greatest day of many of our lives. We four always know how to bring the fun!

Sian, **Cen**, and **Dylan Edwards** — the most wonderfully nutty people we know. We couldn't function without you. Life with you has a unique reality where 30 miles feels like a different distance, elasticated jeans defy fashion norms, WWWAAAHHH attacks are a daily occurrence, and "beefo" isn't the official term for a beef sandwich as one might expect it.

Sarah Feehan — you have taught me that sass is the best default setting to handle any situation. Thank you for showing me the power of wit and attitude; keep inspiring all those lucky enough to know you. You are a powerhouse.

Lex Goodwin — not only my designer but a creative genius. You have given my words meaning and identity through your exquisite use of lines and colour, and our collaboration has forged a forever friendship.

Lindsay, **Matt**, and **Lavinia Griffiths**, and **Soo** and **Gerry Wiggins** — the family we choose. In moments of doubt, you taught me to remember to be royal, and when inspiration is needed, ask the question, 'What would Muriel do?'

Jay and **John Harley-Fox**, and **Bethan Harley** — we love you and thank you for making us all proud and for bringing us Isabelle, Sophia and Jakob. I may be number seven, but you'll always be number one.

Tim Hodges and **Tom Buttress** — Darling! To me, you are the biggest success of our entire school. You knew your dream and followed it. Not many can do what they love full-time. You are simply marvellous, and your husband is divine.

Alison and **Rob Jones** — our best friends whom I met on public transport, but boy, we now travel in style and do all the things that are bad for our health and teeth. Thank you for all the fun that has been and those adventures yet to come.

Liz McMurtry — thank you from the bottom of our hearts for the love and care you have always shown — even when you stopped talking to us and we didn't even notice. This is the only time I will be nice to you or display any kindness, so please don't get used to it. But we do love you.

Fiona Morgan — thank you for always seeing me when I feel I want to fade into the wallpaper. Your resilience in the face of adversity is awe-inspiring, and you are one of the strongest women I know.

Sian Morgan — dearest cousin mine, who looked for the errors so meticulously in the telling of this story. You didn't grumble once. I still remember how you would take me into town on a Saturday as a child to buy me a book. You've always had such a big heart.

Nat and **Rachael** — who were as excited to format my words as I was to have them do it. I highly recommend The Book Typesetters.

Owen Rivers — the greatest Chiropractor who makes sure that the straightest thing about me is my posture. He keeps us well even when the universe has other ideas.

Christopher Tester — thank you for giving my characters a voice. I still can't believe that someone like me would have the opportunity to work with someone as talented as you.

In alphabetical order, I have to say thanks and show love to — **Geraint Davies** (you always bring joy, speak the truth, and offer support), **Andrew Hallett** (your ability to make me laugh until my ribs hurt means I shall never have a need for one of those abdominal toning belts that Anita Harris insists I must have), **Gareth Jones** (if you ever thought before you spoke, life would be boring — you are my protector and you give the best hugs), **El** and **Selina Morgan** (no one makes me laugh like you two, and never was there a more perfect or beautiful couple), **Mrs Sam Morton** (keep bee-ing yourself by bringing happiness with one jar of honey at a time), **Josh**

Pamplin (the only man I shall ever acknowledge as my one true king), **Ian** and **Kirsten Sheppard** (thank you will never be enough, and all you do could fill this book thrice over. Thank you for making sure I'm thought of. Rudy has been blessed with you both), **Daniel** and **Laura-Jayne Venting** (your strength has pulled me through the worst of times. You're hilarious, perfectly matched, and your kids, Rowan and Freya, are the greatest. They bring me endless joy), **Paul** and **Annie Williams** (you make us all proud, and you're both so loved and we will always be family), and **Ruth "Tootsicles" Williams** (my breakfast buddy and confidante — you inspire so many with your resilience and being mean to you is my favourite pastime).

You have all been an unwavering presence in my life, a shield against those who have tried to trample upon me. While you couldn't prevent the pain of their actions, you protected me from their footprints leaving lasting marks and keeping me down. I am forever grateful for your love and support.

In conclusion, this book would not have been possible without the incredible individuals mentioned above and the countless others, especially my beautiful family, who have played a part in shaping my journey. While I may not have been able to acknowledge everyone, please know that your impact on my life and my writing is deeply appreciated. Thank you all for being a part of this extraordinary adventure.

About The Author

Richie Joyce writes so that he may forget, and in order for him to always remember. The art of storytelling brings relief and purpose in facing the challenges of dyslexia and chronic nerve pain in his head and neck, stemming from a bout of shingles. Inspired by his two childhood passions of Christmas and the Victorian era (yes, it is true that he had a childhood crush on Prince Albert, and has never truly grown out of it), he remains devoted to both. The first by way of embodying the ethos; that it's not the Christmas things you do at Christmastime that count, but the Christmas things you do all year through. The second by dedicating himself to restoring his Victorian home, which he shares with a long-suffering partner and an array of Victoriana (which said partner would gladly throw in the bin).